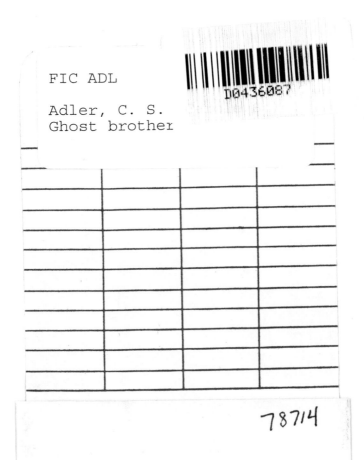

D0436087

78714

Ghost Brother

Ghost Brother

by C.S. Adler

Clarion Books
NEW YORK

Clarion Books
a Houghton Mifflin Company imprint
215 Park Avenue South, New York, NY 10003
Text copyright © 1990 by C.S. Adler

For information about this and other Houghton Mifflin trade and reference
books and multimedia products, visit The Bookstore at Houghton Mifflin on
the World Wide Web at (http://www.hmco.com/trade/).

Printed in the USA

Library of Congress Cataloging-in-Publication Data
Adler, C. S. (Carole S.)
Ghost brother / C.S. Adler.
p.   cm.
Summary: Wishing to be like his older but dead brother, who often
materializes to give Wally advice and support, Wally enters
a skateboarding competition and finally gains the confidence
to be himself.
ISBN 0-395-52592-6
[1. Grief—Fiction. 2. Brothers—Fiction. 3. Ghosts—Fiction.] I. Title.
PZ7.A26145Gh   1990   89-37124
[Fic]—dc20
CIP   AC

BP 10

For Fran and Lauren and Grayson
who loved him, too.

Ghost Brother

Chapter 1

Wally was flossing his teeth at the bathroom sink when his fifteen-year-old brother appeared. It didn't surprise Wally anymore. Ever since the funeral, Jon-o had been showing up unexpectedly. This time he was sitting on the edge of the tub, wearing cutoffs and his favorite T-shirt, the one with a surfer under the curl of a huge wave. "You're stalling," Jon-o accused Wally.

"Yeah, I am," Wally admitted. He turned the water on to keep from hearing his aunt and cousin yelling at each other downstairs.

"So are you going down for breakfast or what?" Jon-o asked in that impatient, big brother voice that usually got Wally moving.

"I guess so. . . . *We'd* never talk to our Mom like Nicole talks to Aunt Flo, would we, Jon-o?" Wally turned the water off and looked at his brother who was jiggling his hairy leg as if his long, muscular body still itched with energy.

"Aunt Flo wouldn't have had an excuse to stay here all summer if you'd gone to day camp with your friend," Jon-o said.

"Yeah, but I didn't feel like it." Wally hadn't felt like doing anything much since Jon-o's funeral a week and a half ago. He turned off the water.

Aunt Flo's know-it-all voice rose from the kitchen. "If that boy's as gone on you as you think, Nicole, not seeing you this summer won't discourage him."

"It will. It will, Ma. And anyway, who're you kidding? You *want* him to find somebody else. That's why you didn't let me stay home with Papa."

"Nonsense!" Aunt Flo snapped. "I came to help my sister in her time of need. And *you're* here to keep your cousin company."

"Oh, sure, Wally needs my company! In case you didn't know, eleven-year-old boys and fourteen-year-old girls don't have *a*-ny-thing in common."

In the bathroom, Jon-o showed his perfect teeth in a wolf grin. "She's right," he told Wally. "You and Nicole don't have *a*-ny-thing in common."

"It's not funny," Wally said. "You always think everything's funny, Jon-o."

"Sheesh!" Jon-o said in disgust and disappeared as instantly as he'd come. He should have kept his mouth shut, Wally told himself. Jon-o never had put up with complaints or criticisms, and now that he was a spirit, he could blip off in an instant. Well, Jon-o had always moved fast.

"You could be more patient," Wally told his brother although he wasn't there to hear. Being dead, where did Jon-o have to rush off to anyway?

Wally wished *he* could get away. Aunt Flo filled their house to bursting with her solid presence. Plus she and Nicole had taken over his bedroom, his and Jon-o's. Mom had tried to convince Wally that he should be glad not to have to wake up to the sight of Jon-o's empty bed. And the den was cooler because it didn't catch the afternoon sun. Okay, but he was cramped in the den with his belongings jammed in boxes between the desk and couch; he liked things in their proper places.

A sudden notion cheered him. After Aunt Flo left, he could spread out his stamp and rock collections on Jon-o's big worktable. He'd have the whole room to himself. Yeah, right, the whole room but not Jon-o. No big brother to guide him, to get mad at, to make life exciting. No Jon-o. Wally gritted his teeth against the ache.

"Wally, your eggs are getting cold," Aunt Flo shouted up the stairs. She had good lungs. Exercised, Wally suspected, from yelling at her eighth-grade classes back in Binghamton. That was where she and Nicole came from, from the countryside near Binghamton, New York, which was more than a three-hour drive west of Schenectady, his town, the place where he had grown up. In

· 3

normal circumstances, Wally only had to put up with Aunt Flo on holidays.

"Coming," he answered. He clumped downstairs, wishing he'd gotten up to eat breakfast with his mother before she'd left for work. He'd meant to wake up early to have some time alone with her, but lately he'd had trouble falling asleep. Last night it had been near dawn, and then he'd overslept.

". . . Your father and I aren't made of money, Nicole. We can't afford these long-distance phone calls. Let him call you," Aunt Flo was saying as Wally walked into the kitchen.

"You can take it out of my allowance if you're so worried about the money," Nicole said.

"What allowance? You already owe us more than you're due to get until September."

Quietly, Wally sat down to his eggs. They were cold. He drank his orange juice, and tried to ignore Nicole who was claiming she could earn money baby-sitting if she were home.

"Nicole, stop whining," Aunt Flo said. "It's a hot day. Why don't you and Wally go over to that big park to swim. What's it called, Wally, Central Park?"

He nodded.

"Where all those dirty little kids go?" Nicole yelped. "I wouldn't swim there for anything. Besides, it's too far to walk."

"Wally, would you like to go?" Aunt Flo asked, plastering

a kiss on his cheek before he could duck. She applied affection with as much determination as everything else.

"No, thanks." Wally waited until Aunt Flo turned away before wiping his cheek on his shoulder.

"You're just going to hang around here all day again?"

"Un huh."

They were both looking at him. His wiry cousin scowled at him behind the drape of her long dark hair as if he were the one who'd trapped her. His well-upholstered aunt was smiling sympathetically; in a minute she'd think up some chore to keep him busy. Aunt Flo believed in keeping kids busy. If only Mom weren't worried about him being home alone while she worked. Or if only Jon-o had died in the winter. Then Wally would have been in school and Aunt Flo would have been busy teaching.

"So how do you feel this morning?" Aunt Flo asked him.

"Fine."

"You could invite some friend over to play with you if you want."

"Nobody's around except Aaron and he's in JCC day camp."

"Well, what else would you like to do?"

"Jon-o was going to teach me to skateboard this summer," Wally mumbled and immediately wished he hadn't.

Sure enough, Aunt Flo announced, "Skateboarding's dangerous."

"Not that dangerous," Wally said.

"Better think of something else. Want to go food shopping with me?"

"No, thanks."

"I'm taking the bus. I could use help with those heavy bags."

"Oh, Mama!" Nicole said. "Leave the kid alone, why don't you?"

"I'm going out to the garage," Wally said.

"Eat your eggs first," Aunt Flo ordered.

"I'm not very hungry, thanks." Wally got up and scraped his plate into the garbage before Aunt Flo could start lecturing him about wasting food. He didn't like to waste food either, but no way could he swallow cold fried eggs. "Excuse me," he muttered and slipped out of the house.

The door of the detached garage was rolled halfway up. Inside it was restfully dim with just enough light to see by.

Jon-o looked like a movie star tough guy sitting astride the chromed-up wreck of a motorcycle he'd bought. Rebuilding it had been one of his summer project plans. Jon-o had been good at fixing things, anything from Mom's old vacuum, to a plugged toilet, to her ailing Plymouth.

"Neat, huh?" Jon-o said. Pretending to rev up the engine, he puffed out his cheeks and made sounds like a little kid. It always shook Wally when Jon-o shifted from the big brother role to acting like a little kid.

"So what should I do with your motorcycle?" Wally asked.

"Do with it? Don't you want it?"

Wally couldn't imagine ever riding that massive machine, much less repairing it himself, but he didn't want Jon-o to think he was still a nerd. A guy like Jon-o didn't want a nerd for a brother. "I'd rather have your skateboard," Wally said. "You were going to teach me to skateboard this summer, remember?"

He must have sounded angry because Jon-o said, "Hey, Wally, it's not like I wanted to die."

"You didn't have to try to save that kid. You didn't even know him."

"Are you going to give me a hard time again?"

"No," Wally hastened to promise.

"Okay then. Get my skateboard down and try it out, why don't you?"

"I kept falling last time."

"You're a year older. Come on, little brother. Life's boring unless you take a risk now and then."

"Not for me it's not boring."

Suddenly Wally realized Jon-o wasn't there anymore. Now why had he gone when they were right in the middle of discussing things? Disgusted probably. "I can't help being cautious. I was born that way," Wally said to nobody.

Doubtfully, he surveyed the garage which was filled with boards and chunks of wood, old doors, windows Jon-o had collected for building a greenhouse, bikes needing a new wheel or gearshift. Above the old lawn mower and the ancient snow blower were shelves of paints and nails and screws. Wally lifted Jon-o's skateboard from the hooks on the wall below the shelves. Jon-o's first board had been homemade, but this one was a real slalom board, wide and sleek with big polyurethane wheels. He'd bought it last summer with money he and his friend Nick had made doing odd jobs.

Wally stroked the skateboard. He remembered Jon-o on it, whipping down the street behind Mom's car and stopping smartly next to her window as she waited for a red light. "Forgot to kiss you good-bye, Mom," Jon-o had said. Startled, she had laughed and told him he was crazy and warned him to be careful, and not to skateboard in traffic. He'd kissed her, and she'd driven off smiling with Wally beside her. Jon-o had been able to make Mom smile at anything. All Wally could get her to smile about were his straight-A report cards. No wonder Jon-o considered him boring.

Energy drained from Wally, leaving him limp. "I'll try the skateboard later," he said in case his brother was listening.

Aunt Flo's round red face showed under the garage door. She rolled the door all the way up and looked around.

"What a mess! No wonder your mother can't get her car in here. You know what would be a good summer project, Wally? Clearing out this junk."

"It's not junk."

"Sure it is. You lug it out to the curb, and I'll call the town about carting it away."

"This was Jon-o's stuff."

"Wally," Aunt Flo said, "hanging onto your brother's belongings won't bring him back. When your father died, the first thing I made your mother do was clean out his closets. It's unhealthy to cling to the past. I told your mother that then, and now I'm telling you."

A sudden urge to punch Aunt Flo took hold of Wally. She rode over everything like a tank. No wonder Nicole was rude to her. "I'm thinking about building a tree house," Wally said, clamping down hard on his anger.

"Well, fine," Aunt Flo said. "Just stay out of trouble." She left the garage door wide open and returned to the house.

Wally pulled the door halfway down again to give himself some privacy. He couldn't build a tree house. Why had he said that? Jon-o had already tried building one in the big tree that leaned into their neighbor's yard, but the police came and made him take it down. No permanent structures, like sheds or tree houses, were allowed because their property was inside the city limits, the police had said. They'd had a complaint about the tree house from the old couple next door who were mad because they believed the Kraft boys had thrown eggs at their windows on Halloween. It hadn't been Jon-o and Wally. They'd just helped with the clean up to be nice.

"They probably figured we wouldn't have helped clean up if we hadn't done it," Jon-o had reasoned, and he'd continued greeting the old couple cheerfully.

"How come you're nice to them when they're so mean?" Wally had asked.

"Staying mad at people just eats your guts out, Wally."

"We could get back at them."

"They're old. They've got their problems."

The truth was, Jon-o had been a nicer person than he was. If one of us had to die, it should have been me, Wally thought.

"So, what are you going to build?" Jon-o asked. He was leaning against his motorcycle now, with his thick brown hair falling in his eyes.

"I don't know. Last summer I did that birdhouse."

"Yeah, it took you forever, but it was a classy birdhouse. You do things right, when you do them. So how about a birdfeeder this year?"

"Will you help me?"

Jon-o laughed. "Hey, I'm just a spirit, remember?"

Wally remembered all right. He'd been so glad the first time Jon-o appeared that he'd reached out to hug him. Clutching nothingness had made him feel as if he were falling. It had been scary, that nothingness. "Why can't you come back with your whole body, Jon-o?" Wally asked.

"You heard the minister say it. My spirit lives. My body's in the ground. It's better than nothing. Better than if we couldn't be together at all anymore. Ah, come on, Wally, cheer up. What would it take to make you smile?"

"Get rid of Aunt Flo," Wally said. It was meant to be funny, and Jon-o laughed. He was the only one who'd ever appreciated Wally's humor.

"I don't feel like doing anything. Not alone," Wally said. He put his hand on his chest where the pain was balled up.

"You're not alone. I'm here. But if you want me to stay, you better start doing something interesting."

Wally noticed that he was still holding Jon-o's skateboard. "You could teach me how to use this, couldn't you?" Wally asked about the skateboard.

"You bet."

"Let's try it then."

Their asphalt driveway didn't have much slope, and it was cracked and wrinkled. Wally set his left foot at a slant near the nose of the board and pushed off with his right. He managed to balance with both feet on the board, bending his knees with his arms out the way Jon-o had taught him. But when he tried to turn at the end of their short driveway, he lost his balance and fell off. It was a nothing fall, and he'd been going too slowly to get hurt. He glanced at the house. Luckily, no one was watching him. He retrieved the skateboard from the gutter.

"Keep at it, kid. Get it going before you put both feet on. We'll have you doing wheelies in no time," Jon-o said.

With his brother watching him, Wally tried again. Eventually, he got the skateboard to turn a little before he slipped off. But he was in the street when, just his luck, Aunt Flo came walking along from the bus stop with two huge plastic grocery bags dangling from her arms.

"Wally Kraft, what are you doing playing with that thing in the street? You want to kill yourself?"

He winced, but she didn't seem aware of what she'd said. "I'm just practicing," he told her. Jon-o, of course, had disappeared.

"Practice safely then. If you must skateboard, wear elbow and knee guards and a crash helmet."

"I'm not doing tricks, Aunt Flo. I'm just learning how to stay on."

"I don't care what you think you're doing. You've got to take care of yourself for your mother's sake. It's enough she's lost one son. . . . I think I saw a helmet in your bedroom closet. Come with me."

There was no evading Aunt Flo. She dumped the bags of food in the kitchen and marched him ahead of her upstairs. The helmet they found was left over from the year Jon-o had played football. It fit Wally fine.

"Now what've you got for your elbows and knees?" Aunt Flo muttered.

"Nothing."

She frowned at Wally. "Is that so? Well, you're not going outside unless you can think of something to use." She stomped downstairs, calling, "Nicole, stop reading and come help me put the food away."

"What about Wally?" Nicole asked.

"He's busy."

Helmeted, with his elbows bandaged in strips from an old pair of jeans, and knee pads from the football era showing below his shorts, Wally presented himself to his aunt in the kitchen. She nodded, straight-faced at first, but when Nicole began to snicker, Aunt Flo's lips twitched. Suddenly she was laughing heartily — laughing at him. Wally was furious. He yanked off the helmet and unstrapped the knee pads. "I'm not wearing this stuff."

"No, Wally, you have to," Aunt Flo said. "I'm sorry I laughed. Nicole set me off."

"You look so goofy!" Nicole said.

"Jon-o never wore stuff like this," Wally growled.

"You're not the natural athlete he was. You need the protection," Aunt Flo said.

Angrily Wally unwound the bandages from his arms.

"I'm not trying to insult you, Wally," Aunt Flo said. "What I mean to say is you're the student and Jon-o was the —"

"Jon-o was a good student, too, when he wanted to

be," Wally said. He stuffed the denim bandages and the knee pads into the helmet and double-timed it back upstairs to shove everything out of sight at the back of his old closet.

"Take it easy," Jon-o said to him when he was knocking aside Aunt Flo's shoes and Nicole's sneakers. "The driveway's not a good place to learn anyway. What you need is a hill. You could go over to Nick's."

That was where Jon-o had learned to do wheelies, practicing on the garage lot next to his friend Nick's house and on Nick's hill. He and Nick had even talked of making money as an exhibition team along with Marie, Nick's sister. She'd been as good an athlete as the two guys last year, when she was only thirteen.

"Maybe I better forget about skateboarding, Jon-o," Wally said.

"Since when did you get to be a quitter? Come on, little brother. Don't I always boast how you never give up once you start something?"

Wally huffed out a sigh. "I don't know, Jon-o."

"You don't know what?"

"You didn't even know that kid. I don't see why you had to try to save him."

"So what was I supposed to do, stand and watch him drown?"

"No," Wally said. Of course Jon-o had had to jump in the water. He wouldn't have been Jon-o if he hadn't. But it was like the cold eggs this morning; Wally couldn't make himself swallow it.

"Jon-o?" Wally called, not sensing his brother's presence anymore. Gone again. "All right. All right. Tomorrow I'll take the skateboard over to Nick's," Wally promised. And then he begged. "Come on back, Jon-o. Please."

Chapter 2

"Now I'm going to sit here until you finish that tuna fish sandwich, Wally," Aunt Flo said. "I'm not letting you waste away to nothing." She lowered her bulk into a chair opposite him at the kitchen table.

"I'm sorry I laughed at you," she added quietly. "I didn't mean to."

"I'm not going to wear all that stuff outside," he said.

"We'll see. . . . Eat your sandwich. . . . You know, your mother's had more than her share of tragedy. She lost your father to cancer when you were only three, and now with Jon-o gone — think what it would do to her if anything happened to you."

Because of the tears in Aunt Flo's eyes, Wally took a big bite of the tuna fish sandwich. Even though he wasn't hungry, he made himself chew and swallow and take another bite.

Aunt Flo wiped her eyes and asked more cheerfully, "So what're your plans for this afternoon?"

He sipped his milk, considering possibilities. Skateboarding would have to wait until tomorrow when he could sneak out without being burdened with extra equipment. Aaron didn't get out of the Jewish Community Center day camp until evening, and then he'd be busy probably. Weekends were likely to be the only time they could get together, and Wally didn't have anybody else he could hang out with.

He wished he'd listened when Jon-o used to give him hints about making friends. It had always been hard for Wally. One reason Aaron and he stuck to each other was Aaron wasn't good at making friends either. Wally was still considering what he might do when Aunt Flo threw in a suggestion.

"I'm going for my five-mile walk. Why don't you come with me?"

"No, thanks."

"Afraid you couldn't keep up?" Aunt Flo grinned.

Wally shook his head. He didn't even want to try.

"Well, maybe Nicole would play a game with you. Monopoly or something."

He tensed. The day after the funeral when Aunt Flo had forced Nicole to play with him, she had sullenly wiped him out at Risk, all the while letting him know how bored she was. No way did he want to repeat that.

"I think I'll plant a vegetable garden," he said hurriedly.

"A vegetable garden! Terrific! Let's make it a family project."

"I helped Jon-o make a garden last year," Wally said. "It was him and me did it all."

"You mean he and I."

"Right. Just us guys."

Aunt Flo snorted. "Have it your own way. I thought it would be more fun to work together."

Stubbornly Wally shook his head. The idea of digging up the old vegetable plot and planting it alone appealed to him. But could he manage it without Jon-o around in the flesh to do the heavy work? He'd better try. Jon-o had done it when he was eleven. Besides, a garden might be the only thing Wally could do as well as Jon-o would have done it.

Filled to capacity with tuna fish, Wally said, "I can't eat anymore."

"One more bite and then you can go," Aunt Flo urged. "— after you finish your milk."

He took a small bite, but even that was hard to get down. The phone rang. While Aunt Flo was answering it, Wally brought his plate and glass to the sink and poured his milk down the drain. It was sinful, he knew, but he'd throw up if he had to drink the rest. Mom would understand. She was reasonable. If you had a good argument, she'd let you win, not like Aunt Flo who thought the only good arguments were hers.

Nicole was lying on her stomach in the middle of the red Oriental carpet in the living room, the one Mom had inherited from her in-laws. His cousin was watching a soap opera. Her head and arms were propped on the big cushion from India that Jon-o had picked for Wally and him to give Mom for Christmas last year. Wally was carefully stepping over Nicole's legs when she startled him by saying, "Watch it!" His toe caught her shin and he tripped and fell on his hands and knees.

"You klutz. How are you going to skateboard when you can't even walk yet?" she snapped.

"Sorry." He slunk into the den and pulled old jeans and his gardening hat from the clothes box under the daybed. Jon-o had given him the hat, which said "Fry's Paints," to match the one Jon-o had worn to do the planting last spring. Their garden had included tomatoes and lettuce and zucchini, parsley, peppers, and peas, plus corn that hadn't grown too well. The tomatoes and zucchini were the biggest successes. Late June wasn't the best time to be starting a garden, but so what? At least digging didn't require a football helmet.

Wally located the spading fork, caked with the remains of last year's mud, in the corner of the garage next to the wheelbarrow. He rolled his equipment through the backyard which was surrounded by overgrown bushes, blooming now with pink bell-like flowers. In the center was the circle of roses that Mom pampered. The lawn surrounding it was pretty patchy. Jon-o used to mow it. Wally guessed he'd have to do that now. For the vegetable garden, Jon-o had dug up a wide strip along the fence at the back of their yard. Giant weeds had taken it over. They needed to be pulled out first.

Wally sweated rivers with every clump of dirt he turned. He stopped to wipe his face dry and was discouraged by how small the turned-over area was compared to the rest even though his hands were already reddening up for blisters. He'd have to look for the gardening gloves, but first he'd take a thinking break and plan what to plant where. It could be a small garden. Jon-o had gotten a kick out of giving away what they didn't need, but Wally didn't know anybody to give a surplus to if he had one.

"What are you up to?" Nicole asked. She'd come outside in a bathing suit and was setting herself up on an aluminum lounge chair next to the roses.

"Making a vegetable garden."

"You're supposed to start in the spring."

"I know, but we didn't."

"You'll never get it turned over at the rate you're digging."

"Hey, Nicole, it's my project, okay?"

She sniffed disdainfully and started slathering sun block on herself.

With her there, Wally couldn't enjoy his thinking break. He gritted his teeth and went back to digging.

Presently the muscles in his shoulders and arms got so heavy he couldn't move them. He kind of expected Jon-o to show up and cheer him on, but he didn't, possibly because Nicole was there. Wally was pretty sure he was the only one Jon-o appeared to, first, because Wally needed him so much, and second, because who else would believe in a ghost and not be scared?

He felt so bad that he put down his tools and headed for the den to lie down. What bothered him was not the muscle aches which he knew were temporary, but the swamp in his stomach. That big eerie, squooshy heaviness that he'd been hauling around ever since the cemetery when they had walked away and left Jon-o behind.

Jon-o's friends, and piles of people Wally didn't know, had stood around listening to the minister's prayers while Jon-o was the center of attention in his coffin with all the flowers. That had seemed proper. But then the minister had stopped talking and everyone turned to go. They'd chatted with each other and just walked away. Mother's tear-washed face was a still white space as she took Wally's hand to lead him off, too. He'd looked back over his shoulder, unable to believe that his brother, who'd always been so full of life, was being left behind on the bare hillside with just dead people to keep him company.

They had stood beside the long black limousine that was to take the family home, waiting for Mom to finish thanking the minister. The man suddenly turned to Wally and said, "I bet you're proud your brother died a hero."

Wally hadn't know how to respond, but it didn't matter because next the minister turned to Mom and poured on more comforting words.

Was he proud, Wally had wondered, sitting in the car beside his mother and across from Aunt Flo and Nicole. He thought of the newspaper article about how the kid had fallen out of the rowboat and been swept toward the lip of the dam. Jon-o had jumped in with his clothes on to save him and gone over the falls with the boy. They'd been smashed against the boulders below and both of them had drowned. There in the limousine, rage had filled Wally at the dumb thing Jon-o had done in giving up his life for a kid who probably wasn't even special, nowhere near as special as Jon-o had been. Amos. Amos Ames was the kid's name. Stupid name.

As soon as he heard his mother's car, Wally got off the daybed and went to the kitchen to greet her. She always seemed a little unfamiliar dressed for work, taller and slimmer than usual in her heels, with her blond hair sleeked back and makeup and earrings brightening her pale face. Mom was a secretary in the college president's office. "Wally," she called and held out her arms. He hugged her hard.

"I'm glad you're home," he said, but before he could tell her how his day had been, Aunt Flo wedged herself between them.

"Let your mother sit down and take a load off her feet," Aunt Flo said. "You look beat, Cyn. How'd it go?

Your first day back at work. It must have been hard."

"Oh, no. Everybody was very kind. They all — you know, made a point of stopping to tell me how sorry they were. A lot of them had been to the funeral. . . . I — I was glad to finally get into things and deal with strangers who didn't know." She stroked Wally's hair back from his forehead. "You look tired, love," she said to him. "What have you been up to?"

"He knocked himself out in the yard," Aunt Flo said. "I got most of a tuna fish sandwich down him for lunch, but he dumped his breakfast in the garbage can."

Wally scrunched down guiltily. So he hadn't fooled his aunt after all.

"What are you doing in the yard?" Mom asked him.

"Putting in a vegetable garden," Aunt Flo answered. "I offered to help him, but he said —" The phone rang.

"I'll get it," Nicole shouted as she ran in from the living room. Her hair was laced in tiny braids around her thin face. Seeing how often she changed her hairstyle, Wally had asked her if she wanted to be a beautician, but she'd told him scornfully that she planned to be an airline stewardess and travel all over the world.

"Barney!" Nicole shrieked into the receiver. She whirled around the kitchen door into the hall, stretching the spiral telephone cord out straight.

"Nicole, you wreck that cord and you'll pay for a new one," Aunt Flo yelled. She got up and yanked her daughter back into the kitchen.

Nicole put her hand over the receiver, to which she was still attached. "Cut it out," she blazed at her mother. "This is long distance. Can't you leave me alone for two minutes?"

"Come into the living room," Mother whispered to Wally. "And you can tell me about the vegetable garden. Jon-o would be proud of you."

"Yeah, but —" Wally was going to tell her he didn't know if he was strong enough and show her his reddened palms, but Aunt Flo bustled into the living room after them.

"So how about if tonight we eat that chicken and rice casserole your neighbor sent us, Cyn?"

"Fine," Mom said. "And then I'll start on those thank-you notes."

"Wait'll you see the mail. The card shops must have sold out on sympathy cards. Jon-o sure was a popular kid."

"Yes, I never knew how highly people thought of —" Abruptly Mother burst into tears. Wally drew back from her. Before Jon-o died, she had always been so calm and pleasant. Even when she was mad, her anger had barely rippled. Now he didn't know how to deal with the violence of her emotions, and was relieved to see Aunt Flo enveloping Mom in her arms. He took himself out to the front stoop.

"It's rough, huh?" Jon-o said sympathetically as he joined Wally on the steps.

Wally swallowed back his tears and nodded. "You were the oldest," he said. "You helped her when anything went wrong."

"Now *you've* got to help her, Wally."

"But I can't, Jon-o. I'm not you."

"Yes, you can, kid. You're my brother, aren't you?"

He was, Wally thought. He'd always been proud to be Jon-o's brother.

The sky looked dramatic with dark blue rain clouds bordered in white above the pointy roofs of the houses across the street. By day, the narrow old houses with their peeling paint and cracked stucco looked shabby, but evening had made them mysterious.

"Can you see the sky?" Wally asked his brother curiously.

"I don't have to. You see it."

"You're just in my head, aren't you, Jon-o?"

"I'm here," Jon-o said. "It's me, and hey, I still love you a bunch."

It was peaceful sitting there on the front steps. When Wally heard Aunt Flo's loud laugh from inside the house, he grimaced.

"Mom needs her here this summer, Wally," Jon-o said.

"But she gets in the way. I can't even talk to Mom with her around."

Jon-o disappeared the instant the door opened behind Wally. "Dinner's on the table," Nicole said. "I had to set for you again, Wally."

"So? I'll do the clean up."

"You better." Nicole sounded strangely cheerful, and she confided, "Barney kept saying how he misses me. Tonight we're going to watch the same TV program and pretend like we're together."

That sounded pretty silly, but Wally didn't say anything as he followed Nicole's narrow back to the kitchen.

". . . If Jon-o'd been older, he might have had an insurance policy to cover the funeral expenses at least," Aunt Flo was saying. "Such a waste, a kid like that with so much potential."

With a smile in her voice, Mother said, "Jon-o was going to be either an airline pilot or a doctor. He asked me just recently if I thought it was possible to do both." She and Aunt Flo laughed.

The phone rang again. Aunt Flo answered it this time. "Cynthia's having dinner right now." She put her hand over the receiver. "It's long distance, Cousin Ann from Arizona."

Mom jumped up to take the call. Her food cooled on the plate while Aunt Flo muttered about sympathy calls and people having no consideration. Finally Aunt Flo bounced to her feet and scraped the chicken mixture back in the dish to reheat in the oven.

He wasn't going to get time alone with his mother tonight, Wally realized as he finished clearing off the table. When the phone was free, he called his friend. "Hi, Aaron. It's me. What are you doing?"

"Making a model."

"Want to come over here?"

"Why don't you come here and help me with the model." Aaron never liked to stop if he was in the middle of something.

Wally hesitated. Aunt Flo didn't drive at night and Mother was tired. "I'll ask," he told Aaron and put the receiver on the table.

"You only have to thank the ones who sent donations or flowers," Aunt Flo was instructing Mom in the living room.

Wally presented his request. "Wally, what's the matter with you?" Aunt Flo said. "Can't you see your mother's worn out? If you want to visit someone we have to drive you to see, do it on the days when I get the car."

"But he goes to camp."

"See him weekends then, and find somebody else meanwhile."

"Mom?" Wally questioned.

A tired frown made a deep crease between her cornflower blue eyes. "Is it really important to you, love?"

"Of course it isn't," Aunt Flo answered for him. "But if you must indulge Wally, I'll drive him. I'm not letting you out again tonight."

"You can't drive with your bad night vision, Flo. I don't mind."

"When are you ever going to learn to take care of yourself?" Aunt Flo fretted. "Even as a kid, you always let people take advantage of you. Anybody wanted something of yours, you'd give it to them. Saint Cynthia's what I'm going to call you."

Mother chuckled. "I'm not even religious."

"So? A lot of saints weren't religious to start with." Aunt Flo had a twinkle in her eyes as if she liked making Mom chuckle. "And you'd look good in a long white robe with a halo. Remember when they made you the Christmas angel in first grade? You were perfect for the part."

Mother smiled. "My halo kept slipping onto my nose."

Nicole joined her on the couch and hugged her. "You're so pretty, Aunt Cyn," she said. "I wish I looked like you."

"Nonsense, Nicole," Mother said, "I'm ordinary-looking. You're the one with style." Eventually Wally understood that they'd forgotten about driving him anyplace. He went to the phone and told Aaron he couldn't come.

· · ·

Mom showed up when Wally was lying in bed that night, staring at the square of sky pricked with starlight. "Awake, darling?"

"Yes."

"Want to talk to me?"

"Sure." He made room for her to lie down beside him.

"Aunt Flo is very dear and she means well," Mother said. "You don't mind having Nicole and her here, do you?"

"I wish it was just you and me."

"Umm. Well, but I have to work, and you didn't want to go to camp."

"I would now."

"It's too late, Wally. Besides, I couldn't hurt my sister's feelings by sending her home and saying we don't need her."

"You could say it nice so that it wouldn't hurt her feelings."

Mom kissed his forehead. "But I *am* glad of Flo's company. She takes good care of me, and I need that right now. Do you mind her so much?"

"She's okay. I just don't like the way she pushes me around. Eat this, do that. She treats me like a baby."

Mother laughed. "She was always like that. She used to push me around when I was a child. I guess I wasn't as independent as you. I didn't resent it very often — Oh, sometimes I must have, especially when I got older and she tried to tell me which boys I should date."

"Jon-o didn't like her much."

"Well, Jon-o never could tolerate being told what to do. He had to be the leader. Even as a little boy, he'd try to take charge." She laughed. "Maybe he inherits that from his aunt —" Her voice went high. "I keep forgetting that he's gone. I guess I just don't want to accept it."

Wally squeezed her hand and whispered, "He's not gone."

"What?"

"He comes to visit me a lot."

"His spirit you mean? I'm not surprised. You adored him. Well, you were so young when your father died. Jon-o filled in for him in a way, didn't he?"

"But I can't touch him when he comes," Wally complained. "And I can't make him stay."

Mother stopped talking then, and Wally realized she was weeping again. He waited patiently. Finally, she dried her cheeks with some tissues. Then she kissed him and whispered, "Sleep well, darling."

"Stay and talk to me, Mom. Please."

"I can't anymore tonight, Wally. I'm so tired. Don't worry. We'll have lots of time together. It'll be just us soon."

After she left, Wally lay watching a crescent moon move through the sky outside his window. He watched it drift from one edge of the window to the other until it finally squeezed out of sight behind the frame.

"So tomorrow I'll go over to Nick's and learn how to skateboard, right, Jon-o?" Wally said into the darkness to coax his brother to come to him. "And you'll help me, right? I'm going to try my best to be like you so that Mom and me won't have to miss you so much. Okay?"

He waited, but sleep came before an answer.

Chapter 3

The blisters made a miniature snowy mountain range below Wally's fingers and hurt when he pressed them. Good thing he was going skateboarding this morning instead of trying to work in the garden again. He got out of bed and listened, but nobody seemed to be stirring yet. What he could do was leave a note saying he was going to a friend's house, then sneak off with the skateboard — a Jon-o-type maneuver for sure.

Even though it was likely to be a warm day, Wally put on jeans and a long-sleeved sweatshirt to protect his elbows and knees some if he fell. He probably would fall. Don't think about it and you won't, Jon-o would say. He'd never told Wally how to stop thinking, though.

Quietly, Wally crept upstairs and used the bathroom. But on the way down again he smelled pancakes, and there was Aunt Flo in the kitchen, flipping one of her golden beauties and smiling at him.

"You're the first one up, so you get fed first, you lucky boy," she said. Her peach-colored robe showed the frilly neck of her nightgown.

"*You* were the first one up," he corrected her, wondering how he was going to get away now. Meanwhile, he sat down to eat amid the jungle of his mother's ferny plants and hanging vines. They glowed in the morning sun. Aunt Flo's pancakes almost did, too. They were even more delicious than his mother's.

"So what's up for today?" Aunt Flo asked.

"Nothing much," Wally mumbled.

"It's Saturday. Why don't you call and see if your friend Aaron's home?"

"It's too early."

"It's after eight," Aunt Flo said. "Don't boys usually get up early?" She smiled at him as if she liked him.

The smile was so warm that he found himself liking her back. "I guess I'll see if he can come over this afternoon," Wally said, and went to make the call.

"We're going to visit my grandmother," Aaron told him.

"Oh," Wally said. "Too bad." He waited but Aaron didn't say anything more. Wally wished Aaron would occasionally make a suggestion about getting together instead of always leaving it up to him. It was as if Aaron didn't care that much one way or the other, as if he didn't need a friend the way Wally did.

"Well, good-bye," Wally said finally and hung up.

He was just finishing his second pancake when the phone rang. It was Aaron's mother. "Wally, how are you doing?"

"Fine." He was wary of the sympathy oozing from her voice. Since Jon-o died, Wally had discovered he was allergic to sympathy. It made him squirm.

"Well, I'm very sorry about your brother. That was such a tragedy."

"Uh huh," Wally said, tasting too much sweet from the pancake syrup.

"Listen, dear, it's important that you have your friends with you at this time, so if you want to come with us to Aaron's grandmother — I'm sure the old people in the nursing home would enjoy another young face. And you and Aaron could visit on the way in the car, like last time."

"No, thanks. I mean, it's nice of you to ask me, but — no thanks," Wally said. He hoped he wasn't being rude, but he hadn't forgotten the day he'd gone with Aaron and seen the toothless old man, sagging in his chair and crying, just crying and crying. Then an old lady with wild eyes had clutched Wally's arm and called him by some other kid's name and commanded him to kiss her. He'd felt bad for days after that visit, bad about himself for not being kind, and bad about the pitiful old people.

"Well, then why don't you come over here tomorrow?" Aaron's mother suggested.

"Okay, sure. I'd like to if you think that's okay."

Aaron's mother assured him enthusiastically that it was.

"So are you going to see your friend?" Aunt Flo asked after the phone call.

"They're going to a nursing home today. I'll see Aaron tomorrow."

"They're going to a nursing home? Why don't you go with them, Wally. Doing something for other people is healing."

"I'm going to see Aaron *tomorrow*," Wally repeated stubbornly.

Aunt Flo raised her eyebrows. "I bet your brother would have gone."

"I know he would, but not me," Wally said. The tears that filled his eyes embarrassed him, but they did shut Aunt Flo up. Yes, Jon-o would have gone. He'd have made the old people laugh and kissed their wrinkles and not been disgusted by the smells. Nothing fazed Jon-o. To become like him meant tearing himself apart and starting over, Wally thought.

"Want more pancakes?" Aunt Flo asked over her coffee cup.

Wally shook his head. "No, thanks. I'm full." He took his dishes to the sink and rinsed them. Then he muttered, "I'm going for a walk. Be back in a while."

Before Aunt Flo could ask where he was going, he ducked out of the house and around to the garage. His stealth was wasted. The garage door growled so loudly going up that Aunt Flo came to peer out the window. He shifted the skateboard to clutch it lengthwise against the hip farthest from the window and ran off. If she'd seen the board, she'd also seen that he had no helmet or elbow or knee guards. He would really be in for it when he got home. At least he should have told Aunt Flo how good her pancakes were. She tried to be nice to him, and he never tried back.

"No sense giving yourself a hard time," Jon-o said, falling into step beside him. "You can't help not liking Aunt Flo."

"But she's pretty nice really, Jon-o. I mean, it's not fair not to like her."

"You worry too much. Didn't I always tell you you worry too much?"

"It's hard to figure out what's right."

"Don't try. Just do what comes naturally."

Wally sighed. What came naturally to him was to figure out what was right.

It was a breezy, bird-chirrupping morning, lively with leaves fluttering and branches swaying and traffic lights winking red, yellow, green. Closer to Nick's house, past the avenue with all the car dealers, the one-way streets were so solidly parked that cars had to thread their way through. Along the broken-up sidewalks were big old dinosaurs of trees that even dwarfed the houses. Jon-o leaped lightly over a gnarled tree root, but when Wally turned to ask him if these trees were Jon-o's favorite scarlet maples, he was gone.

Nick's house was on a dead-end hill next to an auto repair garage and across from an abandoned house. Jon-o and Nick had often practiced on the hill, especially when the garage was open and they couldn't use its sloped parking lot. The only danger was traffic going through the intersection at the bottom of the hill. Maybe if he was lucky, Wally thought, Nick would see him and come out to give him some pointers.

Wally considering knocking on the door and asking Nick for the favor, but he felt shy about it. Nick didn't seem to like him much. Not that Nick was mean, but he'd ask things like, "How many A's you get on your report card, Wally?" Then he would shake his head in disbelief at the answer. "Little Professor," Nick called him sometimes.

"I'm not a brain. Why does Nick always make me out to be a brain?" Wally had complained to Jon-o.

"He just likes to tease," Jon-o had said. But Wally doubted the teasing was friendly. Nick was bony-faced and hard to read, and he rarely smiled.

There were four cars and a motorcycle parked on what should have been the lawn in front of Nick's house. His front porch had been furnished for as long as Wally could remember with a broken chair that nobody used and boxes of empty bottles. The only greenery was a row of tall lilacs that had finished blooming. Nick Bowen had a couple of sisters, a pair of young parents who were always out partying at some bar, and a dog named Spot. Spot was tied up on the porch, the only family member in sight.

Wally checked the intersection for traffic and went a quarter of the way up the hill to start the skateboard. Just the way Jon-o had taught him, he put one foot on the board left of center and kicked off with the other. He slid into the intersection with both feet on the board and his arms out, but couldn't keep his balance and had to jump off before he'd even tried to turn.

"You're doing fine," Jon-o encouraged him. "Just remember to turn your shoulders and *lean* into the turns." Jon-o was standing right in the middle of the intersection where he'd get hit by any car that came through. Except, Wally remembered, Jon-o couldn't get hit because he was dead. Four times Wally made it down the hill okay. The fifth time a car missed him by inches as he zoomed across its path. The driver blasted Wally with his horn, scaring him.

"You better learn to turn or you'll get yourself killed." Nick's deep voice came from behind Wally. He was standing by a motorcycle, holding a toolbox.

"Hi, Nick," Wally said.

"That Jon-o's skateboard you've got there?"

"Yeah."

Nick nodded. "Practice up good and you can try jumping the ditch with my sister Marie and me. We built that landing pad Jon-o designed. It works."

"You jumped the ditch?" Wally was awed. The garage had had to dig the drainage ditch when they blacktopped their parking lot and rainwater running off it kept flooding the Bowens' backyard. The ditch ran the length of the Bowens' property line and was four feet deep and about as wide.

"It's not that hard, Wally. Jon-o did it last year before we had the landing pad."

"He did?"

"Yeah, he nearly broke his neck landing on the dirt, but you know Jon-o. He'd try anything."

"Could I watch you sometime?" Wally asked.

"I might fool around setting up a slalom course tomorrow afternoon. Come by then."

Wally nodded. Then he said, "Jon-o was going to teach me how to turn this thing."

"Want me to show you?"

"Yeah." Wally let his breath out in relief.

Nick took Jon-o's board into his big hands and examined it carefully. Finally, he said, "Jon-o was always breaking boards. This one looks good; no cracks yet and the locknuts are tight." He seemed reluctant to let the board out of his hands.

Wally said, "He bought it with the money you guys made last summer."

Nick's long face split open in a grin. "Yeah — from the money we made painting a lady's garage. Jon-o told her we were expert painters, which was pretty funny considering we were just kids. But we must've done okay because she paid us. . . . You got to check a board first, Wally. Make sure you got enough action in your trucks so you can turn easy. Not too loose, though." His fingers were exploring the metal underpinnings of the board familiarly as he talked.

"Jon-o said you're a mechanical genius," Wally said.

Nick snorted. "That Jon-o was so full of bull." Nick looked up from the board to stare sad-eyed at nothing. "I never saw a guy so full of it." His jaw worked and a muscle in his cheek jumped painfully but he didn't cry. He hadn't even cried at the funeral, although he and Jon-o had been best friends since kindergarten.

"It wasn't bull. He knew a lot," Wally argued.

"Yeah, but not as much as he acted like he knew. He could talk his way out of anything — and not just with girls. You should've seen him in the principal's office a couple of weeks ago. Jon-o'd broken some dumb rule and halfway through his defense plea, would you believe, that bullheaded principal started grinning? Me, I can't get away with anything."

"Me, either," Wally said.

"But what I don't understand," Nick said, "is how it happened. When Jon-o went into the river after that kid, I was so sure he'd save him that I went to find a branch, or something to help them to shore. Then I look and they're gone. They went over while I had my back turned." Nick shook his head. "And I used to think Jon-o was Mr. Lucky!"

I should have been there, Wally thought. If he'd pushed a little harder, Jon-o would have taken him, but Jon-o'd hurt his feelings telling Wally to find somebody his own age and stop being a tagalong. If he'd been there, he could have held Jon-o back. Maybe.

Nick carried Jon-o's skateboard to the top of the hill. He took off like a hawk, riding the board down as if it were attached to his feet, dipping and turning his angular knees from one side to the other. He made a U-turn at the bottom before entering the intersection so that the board was stopped by gravity as it headed back uphill.

"Let's see you try turning now," Nick said.

"From the top?" Wally was scared.

"Midway's okay. Bend your knees like this." Nick illustrated with his feet on the road. "And bring your shoulders around."

Wally tried to imitate him.

"Don't stick your butt out. Bend your knees," Nick said. "Stick your butt out like that and you'll fall on your nose."

The first try went pretty well. Wally's turn was in the middle of the intersection, but at least he'd turned for the first time ever. "Hey, I can do it!" he exulted.

"Good, so practice that and I'll see you tomorrow."

Without another word, Nick got to work on his motorcycle.

It was the sight of the car coming toward him on his left that panicked Wally on his second try at turning. He lost his balance and fell, catching himself on the palms of his hands on the road. The car swished by behind him. Wally stood up shaken.

"You all right?" Nick called.

"Yeah," Wally said. He was too embarrassed to check. But he could still move, so he must be all right. Except when he tried picking up the skateboard, his hands stung. Raw flesh showed and all the broken blisters were oozing bloody stuff. Nick was still watching him, so Wally pretended nothing much was wrong.

He started walking home, trying to figure how to hide his wounds from his mother and Aunt Flo.

By the time he'd stowed the skateboard in the garage, he ached everywhere. Mom's car was in the driveway. The best way to sneak up to the bathroom where he could clean the grit out of his scrapes was to go in the front door — assuming the family was gathered in the kitchen as usual. But he didn't have his key with him. Sometimes Aunt Flo or Nicole forgot and left the front door unlocked, though. Living in the country, they weren't used to locking doors. He allowed himself some whimpering up to the door; then it was self-control time. Lucky. The door was unlocked.

Halfway up the stairs, Wally saw his mother standing at the top. "Wally, where were you? You didn't tell your aunt where you were going. You had us both upset."

From his mother, that was a serious scolding. Wally felt guilty, seeing the vertical frown line dig in between her gentle eyes. Still he stood his ground, knowing if he didn't he'd never skateboard again. "Umm, I went to see Nick."

"Jonathan's friend? Of course. That poor boy must be devastated. Did you talk about Jon-o?"

"Yeah, some. I have to get to the bathroom, Mom."

She caught him at the top of the stairs. "What'd you do to your chin? It's scraped." Her cool hands cupping his face broke him down and he sniveled. "Wally? Did you hurt yourself?"

She screamed when she saw his hands.

"Florence, Florence, come up here and help me," Mom called. She gripped Wally's wrists, horrified by his bloody palms.

It was worse than the time he'd needed stitches and they'd hovered over him in the emergency room of the hospital. Aunt Flo's big body and Mom's slender one crowded his space in the bathroom while they washed his hands and put antiseptic cream on them. They ignored his "ows" and wincing and pulling back. And they didn't stop fussing until they had him bandaged up as if he'd been in a major accident.

"You better have a good explanation for this," Aunt Flo said.

"I just fell," Wally lied, afraid of being forbidden to ever use the skateboard again. "I wasn't looking and I fell in the street and broke the blisters I got yesterday from digging up the garden."

"I'll bet!" Aunt Flo said. "Can't you come up with a better story than that, Wally?"

"Flo," Mom rebuked her sister gently, "Wally always tells me the truth."

"Look at his face." Aunt Flo's eyes were pinning Wally to his lie.

He was blushing. He could feel the heat in his cheeks.

"Wally, why do you look so guilty?" Mom asked.

"I did fall in the street," he insisted and swallowed. If you're going to lie, lie all the way, Jon-o had said. Never change your story in the middle. He had also argued that it was okay to lie to adults for their own good, or so they wouldn't get upset if you'd done something risky.

"Don't you love your mother, Wally?" Aunt Flo asked him ominously.

"Of course I do," Wally shot back at her.

"Wally, don't raise your voice to Aunt Flo."

"I'm sorry, but she makes me mad."

"It doesn't matter if I make you mad," Aunt Flo said. "What matters is that after I told you about using that

skateboard safely, you ignored me. That's willful disobe-
dience."

She had seen him then. Rats! "Mom!" Wally cried in
a last appeal.

"I don't know what I'd do if anything happened to
you," Mom said softly. Her loving look turned Wally to
mush.

"Nothing's going to happen to me," he promised. "I'll
be careful."

Hugging Mom while she held him tight made his aches
throb but he felt that he deserved the punishment. He
hadn't wanted to hurt his mother. She was all *he* had left
in the world, too.

That night when she came to his room to kiss him,
Mom whispered, "I love you so much, Wally."

"Me too, Mom. I love you."

After she'd gone, Wally turned his head and there was
Jon-o sitting on the corner of the desk, sharpening a pencil with a small black sharpener. "What am I going to do
now, Jon-o?" Wally asked.

"Beats me."

"I promised her I'd be careful."

"Yeah. I guess you better sit in the house and take up
knitting to be sure you're safe. 'Course you might stick
yourself with a needle. . . . Mom doesn't understand that
taking chances is part of life, Wally, especially for a guy."

"No, she doesn't."

"So you're going back to being a good little boy?"

"I guess so."

Jon-o kept on sharpening the pencil. He'd always sharpened pencils too far down because he liked the shavings. Wally felt bad. Jon-o wasn't talking; he must be disappointed in his little brother again. Finally, the silence became too much for Wally. "Although what she doesn't know, won't hurt her. Right, Jon-o?"

Jon-o's crooked grin came on like a beam in the dark.

Chapter 4

Wally banged on the bathroom door to remind Nicole he was waiting. If it were Jon-o hogging the bathroom, he could barge in on him. Then Jon-o would smack his butt with a wet towel. Last time that happened, it hurt so much Wally had gotten mad and chased Jon-o, who'd hooted in pretended fear. They'd ended up wrestling on the living room rug where Wally had accidentally caught Jon-o a good one on the nose. "I'm sorry, I'm sorry," Wally had cried. But Jon-o had made light of it.

"You're getting tough, kid," he'd said. "Pretty soon I won't be able to beat up on you anymore."

Wally had been proud to hear it.

"Now I'll never have a chance to get you back. Never," he complained out loud just as Nicole came out of the bathroom. Her slim legs were bare under a long T-shirt. Wally averted his eyes.

"Who're you talking to?"

Evading her question he asked, "How come you take so long in there?"

"Because I'm a girl, and I'm clean," she said in her smart-aleck way.

"It must take lots of washing to get you that way."

"Little beast!" Nicole hissed. She walked off with her nose in the air, leaving behind the perfume of her freshly washed hair. Too bad she wasn't nicer to him, Wally thought. He could like his cousin Nicole.

"Listen," he told an invisible Jon-o in the bathroom mirror. "It's dumb to practice skateboarding with my hands all bandaged up, so I might as well go to Aaron's. . . . You there?" It didn't seem that Jon-o was. Where was he then? In his grave on the hillside? Not likely. He'd hate that quiet place. Besides, to stay put in a coffin in a hole in the ground covered by dirt, Jon-o would have to be really dead.

"You've got to understand," Wally continued arguing after he had spat out the toothpaste and could talk again, "Mom's really sad right now. I have to be extra good for her sake. You would be if it was me that was dead, right?" Jon-o didn't answer. "Okay for you," Wally said finally and went downstairs.

In the kitchen Aunt Flo was urging Mom, ". . . Just a nice Sunday morning drive in the country, Cynthia. You can't sit around mourning him forever."

"I went back to work, didn't I?"

"Well, fine. But this is relaxation I'm talking about. I've never even been to Lake George and they say it's beautiful."

"You take the car and drive the children, Flo. I just don't feel up to entertainment yet."

"But it's two weeks already and life is too short to . . . All right, you said you wanted to visit his grave. We could go to the cemetery. You haven't been back since the funeral, right?"

Mother shook her head. She looked so sad that Wally put his arms around her. She rested her cheek on his head.

"There's a good, sweet boy," Aunt Flo said with such sticky approval that Wally pulled back in embarrassment.

Mother sighed and said, "All right, Flo. We'll go to the cemetery. I'll be dressed in a minute."

The phone rang. It was Aunt Flo's husband. Impatiently, she explained to him how to bake chicken. She usually talked to Uncle Harry as if he got on her nerves and complained that he was too fixed in his routines. Wally wondered why she'd married him.

"You children don't have to come along if you don't want to," Mother said. She'd come downstairs dressed in a pretty print dress. Standing at the door beside her, Aunt Flo looked gross swelling out of shorts and a sleeveless blouse.

"I'll stay here in case someone calls," Nicole said.

"You're going to sit around on a gorgeous day like this, waiting for that boy to call you again?" Aunt Flo sounded indignant.

Nicole pouted. "I hate cemeteries."

"So who likes them?" her mother asked.

"Please, don't fight," Mother said. She looked at Wally who said he wanted to come. He was curious to see if Jon-o would show up there where his body was buried. They waited in the car for Aunt Flo to finish yelling at Nicole, and then they drove to the cemetery.

Aunt Flo was studying the map. "You know you could just about walk it if you took the footbridge over this highway, Cyn. It's not more than a mile and a half as the crow flies."

"I suppose so, but it's a lot more comfortable riding in an air-conditioned car on a day as warm as this."

Aunt Flo stretched, yawning noisily. Then she turned to ask Wally who was sitting in the back, "How you doing?"

"Fine." He wasn't though. It felt weird being on the way to visit his brother's grave on a perfect summer morning. Unreal. I'm doing fine, Wally told himself looking at his bandaged hands. Doing fine. Doing fine. Yeah, sure.

The cemetery looked almost like a park near the entrance where the trees were tall and shapely. Flat cemeteries where gravestones marched off in endless rows were depressing, but this place was hilly and the graves were clumped in groups, family plots Aunt Flo called them. She admired one with a black marble pillar in the center. Wally didn't like any of them. They were too cold, too formal — too dead.

When they finally found the new section where Jon-o was, they saw that someone had dropped a long-stemmed rose on the bare, dug-over grave. Who? Wally asked himself. A girl probably. A girl might buy a single rose like that and leave it for Jon-o.

Mother wept so hard that Aunt Flo had to hold her and pat her back. "There, there, Cyn, there, there, honey."

Wally hoped Aunt Flo was sorry she'd made his mother come. Mom's whole body shook with her sobs, and the awful noise twisted in his gut. He turned his back on the grave and was rewarded by the sight of Jon-o leaning against the nearest tree which was across the road.

"Crummy spot they got me in," Jon-o complained. "No shade."

"You want a tree?" Wally asked him in a whisper.

Jon-o shrugged and answered moodily, "Don't worry about it."

"I'll get you a tree, Jon-o," Wally promised. It seemed like something he could do at least.

They didn't stay long. Aunt Flo and her great ideas,

Wally thought. Mom looked worse after the cemetery visit than she had before.

When he'd eaten enough chicken salad at lunch to satisfy his aunt, he asked his mother if she'd drive him to Aaron's house, but Aunt Flo said she'd drive and told Mom to lie down.

"It'll take your mother a long time to heal," Aunt Flo said in the car as if Wally didn't know. "Your brother was the man of the family. She leaned on him — when he wasn't getting in trouble. Now you'll be the one she leans on."

"I know," he said. She patted his shoulder encouragingly, but it grated on his nerves somehow.

The first thing Aaron's father said when he answered the front door was, "I didn't get a chance to express my condolences at the funeral, Wally. I can't tell you how sorry I am. Your brother must have been quite a guy judging by that crowd at the service."

"Yeah," Wally said. Immediately, his throat choked up and he stiffened against what might come next. He wished he could say he didn't want to talk about it without sounding rude.

"And how are you and your mother doing?" Aaron's father asked.

"Okay."

"Sam!" Aaron's mother pushed his father aside. "Let the boy in for heaven's sake."

"I was about to," Aaron's father said. He had a lot of dignity for such a small man. Aaron did, too.

"What happened to your hands?" Aaron's mother wanted to know.

"Fell and scraped them," Wally said.

She made a sympathetic noise and said, "Well, Aaron's working on his model in the rec room. You go on down, Wally. When you get hungry, there's soda and cake in the kitchen."

"Thanks."

"No smile?" she asked, modeling one of them. "You always had such a nice smile for me."

He didn't feel like smiling, but he would have tried for her if an image of Jon-o's big-screen smile hadn't suddenly flashed in his mind, causing him to hiccup a sob instead. Ducking his head, Wally fled down the half flight to Aaron's wood-paneled playroom. There he stopped to get control of himself. He hoped Aaron's parents weren't mad at him for behaving like a jerk. He liked Aaron's parents.

Aaron's father had set up a workbench for Aaron with all the glues and paints and knives he needed for building his models. The finished models paraded along a ledge below the windows.

"Hi," Aaron said. "I'm almost done." He was putting decals on a gray, gun-laden battleship, using tweezers and a lot of care. Aaron wanted to grow up to be an engineer. His first question to Wally last year in shop class when they'd met was, "What are you going to be?"

"Don't know yet," Wally had told him. He had expected he had plenty of time to make up his mind. Now his course was laid. He would have to become an airline pilot or a doctor in Jon-o's stead. Well, being a doctor might not be bad.

"So how goes it?" Aaron asked.

"Why does everybody ask me that?" Wally grumbled. "I don't know how it goes, and it makes me mad to get asked."

"So you don't have to answer." Aaron put a small plastic flag on the ship. "There. Now it just has to dry. Want to play inside or out?"

Inside Aaron had a slot car racing set and a pool table, not to mention a pile of computer games. Outside was a basketball net over the garage door as well as tetherball and an archery set. Aaron was an only child and both his parents worked. Any toy he wanted, he got. He had even been allowed to invite the whole class to his birthday party. Wally wondered what it felt like to have everything you wanted.

They played Nintendo until Aaron's mother chased them outside for some fresh air. Then they shot baskets for a while although neither of them was particularly good at it.

"My dad wants me to try tennis," Aaron said. "He thinks I have to be able to do *some* sport. He wants me to take tennis lessons on weekends, but I told him five days a week of physical stuff at camp is it for me."

"I'd like to take tennis lessons," Wally said.

"Yeah, well, you can do sports."

"No, I can't."

"Yes, you can. You don't get picked last all the time like me."

"Well, but I'm not good, just not bad," Wally said. "My brother was the athlete in our family."

Aaron gave him a long look. "You talk about him all the time, Wally."

"So?"

"So maybe that's why people ask you how it's going. They figure you must be missing him."

"My mom misses him more than I do. Anyway, she cries more. Sometimes I wake up at night and I hear her crying in the kitchen."

Aaron nodded. "So what do you want to do now?"

"Nothing." All of a sudden, Wally didn't feel like doing anything, not even with Aaron. ". . . I guess I'll go home."

"Already? Don't you want some cake? It's got a fudge nut frosting."

Wally shook his head. "I don't feel that hungry."

"You don't have to be hungry to eat fudge nut frosting," Aaron said.

Wally shook his head again. He needed to be alone because his seams felt ready to burst. "I'll see you next week, okay, Aaron?"

"I guess I could save a piece of the cake for you in the freezer, if you want."

"Yeah, that'd be good. Thanks." He started off.

"My parents are supposed to drive you home," Aaron said. "Anyway, it's too far to walk."

"I can do it. I don't mind." Politely, Wally added, "Say good-bye to them for me, will you? And tell them I'm sorry."

"About what?"

"Oh, you know." He shrugged and left.

He walked a couple of miles before he stopped feeling as if he might cry. It was still early. The Bowens' house was sort of on the way home. He could use his bandaged hands as an excuse for not skateboarding if anyone expected him to. Besides, he didn't have Jon-o's board with him.

The three Bowens and their friends, Hal and Winston, were out on the parking lot behind the auto repair garage. It was an old cinder block, hangar-shaped building with a rounded roof. Vehicles in for repair, or junked and forgotten, were jammed into the flat end of the asphalt parking lot. A new wrecker was parked above the slope that ended at the ditch between the garage and the Bowens' mangy backyard. Bitsy Bowen was perched in a basket hanging from the wrecker's hook, probably some-body's idea of a joke. She was wailing to be let down.

"You hush now, Bitsy, or you'll be in more trouble," Marie told her five-year-old sister sternly. Marie was tall and fair like Nick, but where he was lanky, she was pure grace. She'd had a crush on Jon-o for years before he noticed her just this past winter and began calling her his first lady. She went to a Catholic girls' high school and probably didn't know that Jon-o had had several other girls in the city high school who thought they were his ladies. Or maybe being first was what mattered to her.

Nick was slaloming around tires which had been set up to make a course down the slope. Skinny, silent Hal was practicing wheelies. He'd often shadowed Jon-o and Nick, never saying much, just going along. And Winston from Haiti was leaning, one arm against the wrecker, providing commentary on the scene as usual. Winston had been the one who had helped Nick and Jon-o get the principal's desk up on the roof of the high school last Halloween. He talked a lot.

"How you doing, little Jon-o?" Winston greeted Wally.

"I'm Wally."

"No kidding? I would have sworn you were your brother before he got so big and tough." Winston's eyes twinkled in a friendly way.

"How come you're just watching?" Wally asked.

"Busted my skateboard. Want to hear how?"

"No," Wally said.

"*You* sure in a friendly mood."

Bitsy's mewing became a howl. "Can't somebody let her down?" Wally asked.

"Go to it, boy."

"You're taller than me, Winston."

"Not me. I don't touch that child. She bites." He showed his hand which did indeed have a horseshoe-shaped design of bite marks.

Marie swooped past and stopped by jumping off and catching her skateboard effortlessly. "Don't worry about Bitsy," Marie said to Wally. "We'll let her down soon. She was being obnoxious."

Wally looked up at the tearful girl who sniffled at him hopefully, but he shrugged and left her to her fate.

"How come your hands are bandaged?" Marie asked.

"Fell."

"Nick said you were trying to learn turns."

"Yeah."

"Well, if you want help, bring your skateboard. We're going to be practicing back here on the slalom course."

"Did you leap the ditch yet?" Wally asked.

"A couple of times, yeah."

"This girl's a pro," Winston said.

"It's not that big a deal," Marie said.

"Yes, it is," Wally assured her. "Are you and Nick putting on a skateboard exhibition?"

"That's it!" Winston said. "You got the idea, Wally. We have a skateboarding show and charge admission. Make money. Be the hotdogging, daredeviling ditchjumpers. Only me, I don't jump that ditch."

"My brother did it last summer," Wally said.

"Yeah? You jumping it, little Jon-o?" Winston asked slyly.

"Maybe," Wally said.

"Your mother wouldn't like it," Marie said.

"How do you know?" Wally asked.

"I saw her at the funeral, the way she kept hold of you," Marie said. Dreamily she added, "She's beautiful."

Wally nodded. Something about Marie reminded him of his mother. Marie was more slender and not as moon-pale, but she had the same stillness. "Did you leave a rose on Jon-o's grave?"

"I go over there sometimes after supper," she admitted.

"Ghosts gonna get you, you prowl there at night," Winston said.

Marie tossed her head. "Evening's the best time, when the sun's setting. Ghosts don't bother me."

"Now that's likely true," Winston teased, "you being so ugly-faced."

Marie tried to hit him but he dodged away. Up in the basket, Bitsy laughed. Then she spit, and her spit landed on Wally's arm. He rubbed it off in disgust.

Marie smiled. "So how you doing?" she asked Wally tenderly.

The familiar question felt like a caress coming from her. "Fine. I'm doing just fine," he said.

Nick came by then. "Forget your skateboard, professor? We got an old one you can borrow."

"Not today, thanks." He held up his bandaged hands for an excuse.

Winston told Nick about the exhibition and Nick snorted. "Who'd pay to watch a bunch of show-off kids jump a ditch?"

"I would," Wally said. "I bet Jon-o'd think it was a great idea."

"Probably," Nick said. "You planning on being part of the exhibition, if we had one, Wally?"

"Sure," Wally said.

Nick grinned and slapped Wally's back. "Good. We'll do it then."

Watching them going through the slalom course, Wally thought it wasn't so hard. He could do that. And on the way home, he was pleased when Jon-o fell in stride with him. "I think Nick's liking me better than he used to," Wally said.

"Why shouldn't he like you? You're a good kid."

"He doesn't like guys who play it safe."

"Yeah, well playing it safe's an old man's game. It's great leaping that ditch, Wally. It's like flying."

"I guess next time I'll bring the skateboard," Wally said.

"Yahoo!" Jon-o jumped up and chinned himself twice

on the big limb of the tree under which they were passing.

"Just twice?" Wally teased.

"What do you expect from a guy who's been dead two weeks?"

Wally laughed. Standing on the street corner waiting for the light to turn green, he laughed out loud. Even dead, Jon-o was still fun.

Chapter 5

Monday Mom removed the bandages and Wally decided the raw meat of his palms had healed well enough for him to get back to his garden. He dug out Jon-o's nylon ski mitten liners from the winter glove-and-hat box and used the liners to protect his hands inside the work gloves.

The morning was cloudy and comfortably cool. Wally turned over the clods of earth, working so steadily he didn't even see Nicole until she was beside him asking what he was going to plant. He wiped his sweaty brow with his forearm. "I don't know. Tomatoes and lettuce and stuff like that."

"Basil would be nice. I like fresh basil in salad."

"Okay, I'll put some in." He didn't care what he grew, as long as it was something.

"Want me to help you dig?"

"You?" Wally stared at her in surprise.

"What do you think I am, a couch potato?"

She'd read his mind so well that all he could do was stand there. Silence was least likely to cause a fight.

"Give me that spade, dodo." She grabbed it away from him and began shoving it in the ground with her sneakered foot. "You could get a hoe and chop up the big chunks," she instructed him as she got into the rhythm of digging.

He was tempted to remind her that this was his project and he was in charge, but his palms were pulsing in warning of pain to come. Using the hoe might give them a rest. He got the hoe.

For a while they worked the plot in silence. Then Nicole started talking. "If I were home, I'd be helping out at my friend's farmstand. You should see their vegetable garden! I like stacking the stuff so it looks nice, and waiting on people. They sell corn mostly."

"It's pretty where you live." Wally remembered how toylike the cows and red barns had looked on the humpbacked hills last summer when he and Mom had spent a week with Nicole's family while Jon-o was at Y camp. "I liked that pond we swam at, the one in the farmer's field." Bees had buzzed through acres of clover there and swallows had looped and dipped over the water. It had been a peaceful place.

"Yeah, it's nice. Barney swims there every night after work." Nicole stopped spading and let out a quavery breath. "He'll never be faithful to me the whole summer with all the girls after him. That's what my mother's counting on. Breaking us up is why we're here."

"She came to help my mom, Nicole."

"Oh, bull. That's only one of Mama's reasons. She usually has six for anything she does. Like she also wants to teach Dad a lesson because he wouldn't take her on a summer vacation. And —"

"Why doesn't she like Barney?"

"Because he's eighteen. Also, he's kind of wild. Like Jon-o was."

"Jon-o wasn't wild."

"Tell me he wasn't!" Nicole mocked. "Like he didn't get suspended from school for having beer in his locker this spring?"

"The beer was for a party. Jon-o didn't drink much. He just liked parties. And he liked being in the middle of things."

"So how come your mom was always calling mine for advice on how to control him?"

"You're crazy." Wally shook with anger. "Mom thought Jon-o was great. She just worried sometimes because he had guts and tried things that — well, where he could get hurt."

"He was a big shot who acted like he could get away with anything, but in the end he couldn't."

"Nicole, you shut your big mouth, you —" Wally

threw down his hoe in a fury. He would have liked to hit her. He *would* have hit her if she'd been a boy. "And get out of my garden," he added.

She stuck the spading fork into the loosened soil and said calmly, "I'm just saying what's true, Wally. And I was trying to be nice."

He called her the correct name for a female dog.

She gasped and ran for the house, no doubt to tell her mother on him. He gathered up the gardening tools. The plot wasn't very big, but big enough to start planting. He didn't feel like growing much anyway.

"Wally, come in here. I want to talk to you," Aunt Flo called ominously from the back door.

Wally trudged toward the house, tools in hand.

"Why were you so nasty to your cousin?"

"She said stuff about Jon-o."

"Well, your brother was no saint, Wally. You've got to admit, he had his faults," Aunt Flo said.

"No he didn't. None that hurt anybody."

"He hurt your mother. He made her worry plenty with his recklessness and the way he ignored the rules."

"Just if they were stupid rules."

Stupid rules are made to be broken, Jon-o had said, and when Wally had asked him how you know what rules are stupid, Jon-o had given him an example. Like you couldn't skateboard in the park. They'd passed an ordinance against it, claiming it bothered the dog walkers and young mothers with strollers. But the park had been a lot safer for skateboarders than the streets were. "They could've just restricted us to certain hours or areas," Jon-o had said. He'd gone to the Parks Department to argue about the ban, but they wouldn't change it.

"Wally, you're not listening to me," Aunt Flo said. "Are you going to apologize to Nicole or not?"

"I don't have anything to apologize for."

Aunt Flo looked shocked. "Wally Kraft, you go to your room. What's getting into you? You're turning into a carbon copy of your brother, and I won't have it, hear?" She grabbed his arm to make him answer her.

"I hear you," he said.

She let go. He stowed the tools in the garage. To get to the den, he had to pass through the living room where Nicole was reading. She looked at him as if she expected him to say something, but he wouldn't.

He threw himself down on the daybed. Now what? He wasn't tired enough to sleep again. The clouds had passed and outside the June day glowed green and enticing. He'd never apologize even if he was stuck in this dim closet of a room all day.

"Climb out the window," Jon-o said.

"Then Mom will get mad at me for disobeying Aunt Flo."

"Wally, that bossy lady'll flatten you if you don't stand up to her."

"How?"

"Me, I'd leave her a note and take off."

Wally considered what to do. The more he considered, the more injured he felt. After all, Nicole had started it. Finally, he wrote: "Nobody's got a right to say bad things about my brother, and it's not fair to punish me." He left the note on his bed.

He'd get back by five thirty when Mom got home from work, but he knew she would be angry with him. He hoped he could talk fast enough to make her understand. The screen lifted out easily. He dropped into the bed of lilies of the valley on the shady side of the house. Luckily the fragrant white flowers were gone, and their green leaves were too tough to kill. Once on the ground, he stared at the next-door neighbor's blistered and peeling siding and wondered where to go. Aaron would be at day camp. None of the kids he knew from school were likely to be around. Would anybody be at Nick's house? Not Nick himself. He always had a job in the summer.

The skateboard, Wally thought. He would spend the afternoon practicing turning and stopping. The garage next to Nick's house would be in operation, but his hill would be all right to practice on. Wally crouched to keep his head below the window and circled around the garage. Luckily, he'd left the noisy door partway open. He squeezed under, grabbed the skateboard, ducked out, and ran. No gloves, no guards for his knees or elbows, not to mention his head. He'd have to be very careful not to hurt himself. Mom wouldn't be inclined to take his side against her sister if he came home bleeding again.

Nick's house appeared to be deserted. Bitsy's tricycle was in the yard and Spot whined at Wally from the porch. "Some watchdog you are," Wally said, stroking the dog's bony head. Spot was white and smelly with one black blotch on his skinny left flank. He kept nudging Wally with his nose and wagging his tail. Finally, Wally told the dog, "I got to go now."

The intersection at the foot of the hill had a lot of traffic on it. Wally was tempted to take one run down anyway. Then he got a brainstorm. What about the cemetery? It'd be a lot safer there. It would be a long hike, but the cemetery was closer from Nick's than from his own house, and there was no point going home now.

Purposefully, Wally began walking. He passed a bunch of kids playing ball in an empty lot, but he didn't know any of them. He passed a house where a white plaster saint in a blue plaster alcove held out cloaked arms to passersby. Little kids were splashing merrily in a plastic swimming pool behind a chain-link fence. Then came the high school where Jon-o had gone. In the fall, his class was going to plant a tree there in his honor out near the parking lot. Wally had asked Mom to tell them Jon-o liked maples that turned scarlet best.

"Where are you, Jon-o?" Wally asked, wanting company. He was practically to the cemetery and Jon-o still hadn't joined him. What a pain! The only advantage of Jon-o's death was it should have made him more available. Unless he was waiting at the cemetery. Wally crossed the footbridge and rested awhile above the highway, watching the lanes of traffic blip by in both directions beneath him. A kid in a station wagon waggled his fingers in his ears and stuck out his tongue at Wally.

He was tired by the time he reached the cemetery. Past the stone pillars at the entrance it was kind of peaceful and shady; so he sat down on the first stone bench he came to for a rest. Hills full of trees and graves blocked his view, but Wally knew Jon-o's grave was to the right. At least that's the way Mom had driven.

At the top of the first rise, he set the skateboard down and shoved off. It was a nice run past the heavy stones marking each small square neatly planted with grass or ground cover. No cars in sight. He tried a turn. To his surprise, he was able to twist his upper body and shift his weight smoothly from his right foot back to his left heel as he came out of the turn. Eagerly, he lugged the skateboard up another road to the right.

Most of the flowers left on the graves were fake. Too bad he hadn't brought some fresh ones for Jon-o. By now, the rose Marie had left would be dead. "Jon-o," Wally called softly. "Where are you anyway?" It occurred to him that if Jon-o's spirit was so lively, there might be other peoples', strangers', hanging out there in the cemetery where their bodies were, but he didn't sense any. Good thing, too. A bunch of unfamiliar ghosts on the loose would be scary.

At the top of the next hill, Wally surveyed the land-scape. It was like a miniature city, but instead of houses, each lot had a gray or white or maroon stone with carv-ing on it. He'd thought he remembered where Jon-o's grave was, but coming in on foot had confused him. There was a building to the left with a couple of cars in a parking lot out front that he didn't remember seeing before. Maybe he was lost. Two men near a pickup truck with gardening tools in the back were planting ivy around an obelisk engraved with names. Wally pushed off on the skateboard to sail down to the men and turned smartly at their truck.

"Hey, kid, you can't play here. Get out." The stocky man was dark-browed and snarly.

"I was looking for my brother's grave," Wally said. "It's around here somewhere. It's pretty new."

"Who'dya think you're kidding? Get out of here." The dark-browed man advanced on Wally threateningly.

His partner was lank-haired and gaunt. "Was there trees?" he asked Wally patiently.

"No. It was on a hill, but it was bare."

"That way," the gaunt one advised. "That's the new section."

"No playing," the other one said, frowning. "No play-ing in the cemetery."

Cautiously, Wally carried the skateboard past the man. As soon as he'd turned the corner and come upon the rangy hemlock at the bottom of the hill, he recognized where they'd stood with the minister. The rose was gone. The rectangular square of earth that weighted down the coffin lid still looked raw and ugly there where Jon-o had been left. Wally wondered how soon the gardeners would get around to planting stuff here so it wouldn't look so bare. He tried to imagine his brother's agile, broad-shouldered body rotting in the ground. How long did it take for a body to rot anyway? Suddenly he hurt as if a pound of cold iron had been slung in his gut.

"Jon-o," Wally whispered. "You're not really there, are you? You can't be. Not you. Come on, Jon-o. Where'd you go? Don't hide on me, please!"

Wally shuddered. Hot tears spurted from his eyes, and his insides wrenched unbearably. "Jon-o?" Wally begged one more time before he flung himself on the skateboard and went barreling madly down the hill, too fast, out of control. He skidded at the bottom. Trying to avoid the gardeners' truck, he fell hard on his hip and arm. The side of his face scraped the roadway.

The gaunt man picked him up. "You break anything, kid?"

"Kid's trying to kill hisself," the dark-browed man grumbled. "Like we don't got enough dead people here. I told you he didn't have no brother."

"I do," Wally protested. "I do have a brother." He grabbed the skateboard, pulled away from the hand steadying him, and ran back toward the entrance. His arm and face and hip stung, but nothing was broken, and now he needed the comfort of home. He hiked back, pushing himself with determination, ignoring all his inside and outside aches, immune to the curious glances of the people he passed.

On the other side of the footbridge, Jon-o fell into step beside him.

"Mom'll be shook when she sees you. What're you going to tell her?"

"Oh, leave me alone," Wally said. "It's your fault for dying."

"My fault, huh. Well, I'm sorry, Wally, but it was an accident. You can't blame anybody for accidents."

"You should have tied a rope around yourself when you jumped in."

"Yeah, I should've, but there didn't happen to be one lying around. . . . I'd rather be alive you know. I really liked being alive."

"I know," Wally said contritely. He felt his spirit collapsing under the lead weight of Jon-o's death. He just couldn't carry it anymore. He couldn't carry it and he couldn't get rid of it. He wished he were dead himself. It would be easier than trying to be the all-around guy Jon-o had wanted him to be. Easier than trying to be another Jon-o.

Chapter 6

He was hoping for better luck this time in getting up to the bathroom to soak his bloodied shirt in the sink and put Band-Aids on his scrapes before Mom or Aunt Flo or Nicole saw him. He got the skateboard back in the garage all right, then slipped in through the front door and upstairs. They didn't hear him at first because they were laughing it up in the kitchen. A good sign, their laughter. It meant Mom couldn't be too upset about his prison break. Unless Aunt Flo hadn't told her.

Probably it was the plumbing that gave him away. In the kitchen they could hear water gushing down the pipes from the upstairs bathroom.

"There you are," Mom said, opening the bathroom door without even knocking, which she never did. "Where were you all afternoon, Wally?"

"Walking."

Her eyes took in his scraped cheek and she gasped. "What did you do to yourself this time?"

"I just fell again, Mom. It's no big deal."

"Were you using that skateboard after I told you not to?"

"Mom, you don't understand. There's things I have to do."

"No, I don't understand. I thought you loved me, Wally. I thought you had some concern for my feelings. Now look at your face! I'd better take you to the emergency room."

"It's nothing. It just needs washing," Wally protested.

"Be quiet." She was so upset that her fingers trembled icily on his face as she dabbed at him with a clean damp washcloth.

Next Aunt Flo barged into the bathroom. "Here, let me." She took the cloth from Mom's hand. "You get out the antiseptic. It's not as bad as it looks, Cyn. We can take care of it."

Wally would rather have had his mother do the nursing, but he didn't complain even though Aunt Flo was a little rough — deliberately he thought. "Serves you right," she snapped at him when he ouched and owed. "*How* you could do this to your mother after the last time, I don't know. If you were my kid, I'd wallop you good."

"It was an accident," Wally said.

"That could have been avoided if you'd stayed home and done what you were told," Aunt Flo concluded.

"Flo, thanks for patching him up for me," Mom said. She had calmed down. "I'd like to talk to Wally alone now."

Aunt Flo straightened up. "Fine, talk to him. But you better know that he disobeyed me and sneaked out the window after I confined him to his room for calling Nicole a name. It's time you cracked down on this kid, Cyn, or —"

"I'll take care of it," Mother said.

"Well, if you're as easy on him as you were last time, he'll never stop. If he were my kid —"

"But he's not," Mom said with a flick of temper which she tried to cover with a smile. "He's mine."

Wally was delighted when Aunt Flo turned on her heel and marched out.

"Now I've insulted my sister, and what for?" Mom complained. "She's right, Wally, you have gotten out of control."

"I'm sorry, Mom. I'll be better from now on."

"Why did you fight with Nicole?"

He shrugged. "She bad-mouthed Jon-o."

"And why didn't you obey your aunt?"

"Because it wasn't fair. I didn't do anything. Nicole deserved what I said to her."

"Wally, when an adult in authority punishes you, it isn't up to you to decide whether they were fair or not.

If you thought your aunt was wrong, you should have waited until I got home and come to me. Besides that, you got hurt on that dangerous board again."

"I'll be careful."

"You'll be careful, and you will not use that skateboard again."

"Never?"

Mother hesitated. "Not until you get a lot older anyway."

"But I was just getting the hang of it. Everybody falls and scrapes themselves sometimes. It's not that big of a deal. You don't want me to be a sissy, do you?"

"Whoever said you were one?"

"Jon-o used to tease me about being cautious. He said a kid didn't have to be good all the time, just when it counted."

"Jon-o and you had different natures, Wally. You mustn't try to make yourself over in his image."

"Why not? He was a great guy."

"He was, but he had his faults. He was impulsive, while you're a person who thinks ahead more, and that's good. He also had a lot of natural athletic ability, while you and I are not particularly physical."

"Yes, I am. Well, a little anyway. I'm not like Aaron. He can't even hit a ball or run or anything," Wally argued.

Mom brushed his hair off his forehead and said, "Nevertheless, you're the only son I have left, and I want you in one piece. No skateboarding, darling. No anything dangerous. You must promise me." Her lily face wrung his heart. "I know it hurts you that Jon-o's gone. I know you miss him, Wally, but we have to learn to live without him."

"Mom, you don't understand. It's bad to be a wimp. I'll hate myself if — please, let me use the skateboard. I promise I'll be careful."

She shook her head. He looked at her pleadingly. "Mom?"

"No," she said. "The promise I want from you is to stay off it."

"I can't. I can't promise that."

She stiffened and said coldly, "We'd better talk about this some other time when we've both calmed down."

In uncomfortable silence, they ate the spaghetti dinner Aunt Flo had prepared. She wasn't talking, probably because she was angry at Mom. Mom was upset with Wally. Nicole was sulking, and Wally was brooding. He needed to use the skateboard. He needed to take Jon-o's part in the exhibition. Jon-o had been a hero. What was Wally going to be if he listened to Mom and Aunt Flo and never took any risks? Wally the wimp, no doubt about it.

Doing the dinner dishes with Nicole, he could hear the hum of Mom's voice in the living room and guessed by the placating tone she was trying to make up with Aunt

Flo. He wiped the table while Nicole stacked the dishes in the dishwasher.

Abruptly she said, "Listen, I'm sorry I made you mad. I shouldn't have teased you about Jon-o. I know how you felt about him."

"Jon-o was never bad. He didn't cheat or steal or hurt anybody," Wally said.

"I know that. I was just trying to get your goat."

"Well, you did."

"I had a crush on him myself," she confessed. "I guess half the girls he met did. He was sexy. . . . So are we friends again?" Nicole asked.

"I guess so," Wally said, although he hadn't known they were friends before.

"Good, then will you do something for me?"

"What?" He should have known her apology would cost him.

"Barney's coming. Would you cover for me while he's here?"

"Huh?"

"He's coming on the bus this weekend, and we're going to spend Saturday together. Then he'll camp out in the backyard of a guy he knows until he can get a bus home Sunday. But I don't want Ma to know that I'm seeing him."

"I can't lie to her, Nicole."

"You don't have to. You and I can go to the park to-gether, and then you can do what you want — so long as you don't go home — and then we'll meet, you and me, and go back together."

"What if it rains?"

"Oh, Wally, you're such a worrywart. If it rains, we'll go to the mall, or someplace instead of the park."

"The mall's too far."

"We'll take a bus."

He thought about it. It was going to be very inconvenient not to be able to go home all day. What was he supposed to do with himself while she was with Barney?

"Well?" she urged.

"I don't think so," he said.

"You won't help me?" She sounded angry.

"Well." It was awkward to explain, but he wanted to be honest. "I don't see why I should do you that big a favor. You haven't been all that nice to me, Nicole."

"You deadhead! I bet your brother would have done it. I bet he didn't count up what people owed him before he'd do them a favor. He was a generous guy. *That's* why he had so many friends."

It was true, Wally admitted to himself in shame. He wasn't generous, and he didn't like everybody like Jon-o did, and no, he didn't have many friends. "Okay, okay," he said. "I'll do it."

His change of heart didn't stop her from glaring at him. "Fine," she said loftily.

He retreated to the TV set and hunkered down to

watch it. Mom and Aunt Flo seemed to have made up. They were chatting together in the den while Mom worked on her bills at the desk. Nicole had gone upstairs to do whatever she did when she shut herself into her bedroom. The house was full of people, but strangely enough Wally felt lonely. He used to enjoy a rainy day working on his stamps, or going out to look for more rocks to add to his collection. Now he didn't like himself enough to want to be alone. "Jon-o," he whispered. "Hey, Jon-o."

It wasn't as if his brother had sat around keeping him company. Most of the time Jon-o had gone off somewhere with his friends. If he did stay home, he was usually fixing something in the garage, where Wally didn't go because Jon-o was likely to turn him into a gofer or get him to stand and hold something. Being a human clamp was the worst. Wally hadn't liked running errands much, either. And Jon-o was always borrowing money from him, sometimes without permission. Plenty of times Jon-o had made Wally mad, and they'd fought. Jon-o never stopped stirring things up. That's what he missed the most, Wally thought — his brother's liveliness.

He dragged himself off to bed early. His face and arm stung, and he had a hard time finding a comfortable position in bed. The window was open. There were rustlings outside, as if the bugs and birds and little animals were busier in the dark than in daylight. Being outside at night was interesting. Jon-o had liked walking then. One midnight he'd awakened Wally, and they'd slipped out of the house and walked for a couple of miles, talking about life and the universe and whether man was special in it. "At least human beings are important to each *other*," was how Jon-o had resolved it.

The house was quiet tonight. No sounds at all, not the bed squeaking up in Aunt Flo and Nicole's bedroom, no TV murmur. They must all be asleep. Wally lay wide awake. A cold glass of milk would taste good. He padded to the kitchen and was startled by a white shape near the window.

"Mom? What are you doing up?"

"I'm not sleepy, Wally. Why are you up?"

"I'm sorry I upset you. Really I am, Mom."

She held out an arm, and he snuggled against her, something he was too embarrassed to be caught doing in daylight. In the backyard, black branches were thickly scribbled against an ink-blue sky.

"Look at all the stars out there," she said.

"Oh, yeah." And he quoted, "Ranconcomus, Lumarious, and Ignatz."

She laughed softly at the phony star names Jon-o had made Wally memorize one summer night when Jon-o had pretended to know them all. And then her laughing became crying, the painful weeping that made Wally feel so helpless. "I'm sorry, Mom. I'm sorry," he kept saying.

"I miss him so much," Mom said. "Isn't it amazing,

Wally, that one person could fill so much space and leave such an emptiness behind him?"

"Yeah," Wally said.

"They say time heals. I don't know. I still miss your father, and it's been years since he died. . . . Well, it doesn't hurt as much or as often, I suppose, but . . . it makes me feel like an old, old lady to have lost so many loved ones."

"You're not old, Mom. You're still young and pretty."

She hugged him. "I should have *made* you go to camp," she said. "It was a mistake to let you hang around the house all summer. Your aunt means well, but she never had any sons."

"She's not too good with daughters, either. Nicole's mad at her."

"You mean because of her boyfriend? But Flo was right to separate them. He's got some notion about Nicole and him being like Romeo and Juliet. Nicole's too young for a serious romance."

"Nicole says Aunt Flo's also staying with us because Uncle Harry won't go on a vacation with her."

Mother giggled. "Well, she won that one. Uncle Harry says he's game for the western trip now. He's tired of fixing his own meals."

"So is she leaving?" Wally asked hopefully.

"No. She said as long as I need her, she'll stay. She really does love us, Wally. She's my big sister, like Jon-o was your big brother. I was a shy, scared little girl, and your aunt used to fight my battles for me. Remember when Jon-o tackled those kids who stole your bag of candy one Halloween? Flo did the very same thing for me when I was little. If I wanted something, I'd tell her and she'd try to get it for me. I love her very much." Mom sounded apologetic.

"I don't see why they have to stay the whole summer, though."

"Oh, I don't know. We might drive them home on my vacation, and stay with them there for a few days."

"I thought we were going to the beach."

"Without Jon-o?" Mother sighed. "It wouldn't be much fun."

"Why not? You could bring a friend. That lady you work with?"

"Jan has a husband. She couldn't get away."

"So, you know other people you could ask, don't you?"

"You really want to go to the beach so much?"

"Well, I still want to go a little. Don't you?"

She considered for a minute before she said, "Since Jon-o died, I haven't wanted to do anything, not even get up in the morning."

"That's because you're not sleeping at night," Wally said quickly.

To his surprise, she laughed. "Sometimes you remind me so much of your brother," she said.

She couldn't have pleased him more. "How?" he wanted to know.

"Well, Jon-o didn't mope around. He figured out how to fix things and set to work. He made the best of everything. . . . We'll see about vacation, Wally. Meanwhile, we'd better try getting some sleep."

At the door to the den, he said, "We had a good talk, didn't we, Mom?"

"Yes. I guess Aunt Flo will say I've let you off too easy. But I know you mean well, Wally. Just go back to being a good boy, please."

"Yeah, okay," he said. "And if you don't want to go to the beach, we don't have to, but can't we vacation somewhere besides Aunt Flo's?"

"I'll think about it." Mom kissed him and touched his scraped cheek. "And you think about other ways to entertain yourself besides skateboarding."

"I went to the cemetery this afternoon," Wally said.

"You went there alone?"

"Yeah, I walked. Jon-o's grave looks awful, Mom. I think it needs a tree or something."

She put her fingers to her lips, and instead of responding to his idea, she blurted out, "Oh, Wally. I'm so sorry."

"About what?"

She shook her head and kissed him. "Go to bed," she said, upset all over again. He went.

"Jon-o," Wally whispered in the dark of the den.

"Jon-o, Mom feels so bad. Can't you come back for her somehow?" He listened for an answer, but Jon-o wasn't there. "Jon-o, hey!" He sure wished he knew how to reach his brother when he wanted him and not just when Jon-o was willing to be reached.

"Hey, listen, I'll try and get you a tree. Okay? And I'm sorry I didn't help you more when you were here. I'd hold stuff for you now, Jon-o. Anytime."

Wally shivered as the misery crept in. He shut his eyes against it and tried to squeeze it out, but it wouldn't go, not for a long time, not until he concentrated on something else.

Tomorrow he'd call the cemetery and ask about the tree. Tomorrow morning first thing. As for the skateboard, that would have to stay in the garage for a while. Anyway, until Mom felt better.

Chapter 7

It took a couple of days before Wally realized that
Jon-o wasn't coming anymore.

At first, he didn't notice because he was so busy with
the vegetable garden. Tuesday evening he and Mom and
Aunt Flo and Nicole went to a nursery and bought flats
of well-started vegetables on sale. Since each of them
picked what he or she wanted, they ended up with Rut-
gers and Big Boy and cherry tomatoes as well as two
kinds of lettuce, parsley, squash, peppers, and herbs —
enough for a garden twice the size of the one that Wally
had prepared.

He and Nicole got the plants in the ground on Wednesday just at the start of a three-day rain. The tomatoes shot
up so fast in the rain that Wally went out in swim trunks
to stake them. Coming back he gave Nicole and Aunt
Flo a laugh by falling over a pail of water Aunt Flo had
left at the kitchen door for him to wash the mud off his

feet. He didn't see what was so funny. By then he was worrying because Jon-o hadn't shown up in four days.

Probably Jon-o was disgusted with him for giving up the skateboarding, Wally decided. Alone in his room, he tried to reason with Jon-o about it. "I promised Mom," was Wally's basic argument.

The rain kept him involved in a two-afternoon-long Monopoly marathon with Nicole, which she won. The rest of the time, if he wasn't reading, watching TV, or listening to the monotonous downpour, he was stewing about where Jon-o was.

Finding out about a tree for Jon-o took the whole of one frustrating morning on the phone. When Wally finally got connected to the right person in the cemetery's office, she read him a long list of rules. The tree had to be an evergreen, not the maple he wanted because it would drop leaves that would add to the gardeners' work. Then the tree had to be placed according to the cemetery's landscaping plan. Worst of all, it had to be bought through the cemetery office at an outrageous price.

When Mom heard him out about what he wanted to do and how much it would cost, she winced. "It's a lovely idea, Wally, but we're way over budget right now. Let's wait until next year, okay?"

It wasn't okay. He decided to earn the money himself and went door to door in the rain asking the neighbors if anyone wanted to hire him for yard work. Unfortunately, no one did. They either did their own work or hired high school kids.

By Friday, Wally was frantic about Jon-o's nonappearance. In the past, Jon-o had punished him by not talking to him, but never for a week. Once it had happened when Wally made a fuss because Jon-o had raided his piggy bank without permission.

"I'll pay you back with interest," Jon-o had sworn and made Wally suffer by not talking to him until days later when Jon-o had dropped a ten-dollar bill in his lap.

"That's more than you took," Wally had protested.

"Told you I'd pay you with interest," Jon-o had said, making Wally feel cheap. He'd had a hard time convincing himself he had been right to be angry because Jon-o hadn't asked for permission. Suppose Jon-o's absence now had something to do with money, with not being generous?

"I'll put everything in my bank toward the tree," Wally promised in the middle of the night when he couldn't sleep. Still, no ghostly presence came to enliven the darkness.

Did it have something to do with Mom then? Maybe Jon-o thought Wally wasn't doing enough to cheer her up. No, it had to be the skateboard. "She's afraid to let me use it," Wally said. "I can't practice. It'd be really bad if I did that to her now when she's so sad." But it sounded like an excuse when he said it. Jon-o would somehow get around the ban, Wally admitted to himself.

The most frustrating thing was that his arguments and reasoning remained one-sided. Jon-o never answered back, didn't come, just left Wally to stew.

Friday night at the supper table, Aunt Flo said, "The rain's stopped. Let's do something together tomorrow. There's a craft fair in Saratoga that sounds pretty good. We —"

Nicole interrupted her to say, "Sorry, but Wally and I are going to the park tomorrow."

"You can do that any day of the week," Aunt Flo said.

"But —" Nicole was thinking so fast Wally could practically hear her brain humming. "There's a skateboard competition Wally wants to watch and — we're going to take our lunches and maybe use the paddleboats and — just hang out in the sun."

"You and I can go to the fair, Flo," Mother said. Aunt Flo had a passion for craft fairs. Mostly she bought owls. She had owls made out of every material including feathers perched in unlikely corners all over her house.

Lying awake that night, Wally decided that tomorrow, after going to the park with Nicole so it wouldn't be a lie that they'd gone together, he would leave her with her boyfriend and go to Nick's. That was it. And maybe he could practice on Nick's skateboard. If he had to, he'd try the leap over the ditch, anything to make Jon-o return.

Saturday morning the sun shone and everyone was cheerful. But the mothers got anxious when it was time to part and peppered Wally and Nicole with warnings. They were to stay out of trouble, not talk to strangers, take a cloth with them in case the picnic table they ate lunch on was dirty, not get too much sun, and if anything happened they were to call home at once. "We'll be back by early afternoon," Mom said.

"Well, we don't expect to be back before dinner so don't rush for our sakes," Nicole said.

They boarded the city bus across from the post office and sat down side by side. Wally asked her how Barney was going to find Central Park when he got to Schenectady.

"He's got a mouth. He'll ask."

"But it's a long hike from the bus station, and it's a big park. You could miss him."

"Relax, worrywart. He'll find me." She opened the lunch bag and told him to take out what he wanted for his share. He stuffed a tuna fish sandwich, some cookies, and a banana into a plastic bag.

"Where are you going to spend the day?" she asked him.

"At Nick's house."

"Well, whatever happens, don't give up and go home early."

"Why? I could say we got separated," Wally said.

"Then they'll wonder where I am and send a posse out after me."

"All right. Maybe I'll get a bus to the mall or something."

"Here." She handed him two dollars. "For emergency transportation. You don't have to give it back, either. I really appreciate this, Wally. You're okay."

He nodded with satisfaction. His mother wouldn't approve of how he was helping Nicole, but Jon-o would have.

They got off the bus near the park entrance by the rose garden. "See," Nicole squealed. "I told you he'd find me."

The fellow sitting on the first bench in the rose garden could have been her brother, Wally thought. Barney was thin and brown-haired with a narrow, high cheekboned face. He held out his arms and Nicole ran into them. They kissed hungrily, so totally absorbed in each other that Wally, who'd been waiting to be introduced, realized he wasn't going to be. Nicole had forgotten he existed. He wondered if she and Barney could spend the whole day kissing. Suddenly, he didn't feel quite so pleased with himself. Aunt Flo would be furious if she ever found out that he'd helped her daughter connect with Barney. Well, it was too late to reconsider.

. . .

A great clanging was coming from the auto repair garage at the top of Nick's street, but not being able to use the garage's lot wasn't keeping the Bowen kids from skateboarding. Here came Marie, streamlined as a hood ornament, wedeling down the hill with her knees bent and her arms winged out.

She jumped off inches from the cross street and

scooped up the board on the run. Her blond hair fell neatly into the curve of her cheek as she walked toward Wally. He heard the rumble of wheels and watched Nick coming snake-hipped down, not even using his arms for balance. The board seemed pinned to his sneakers. It left the roadway to flip up as Nick curved from one side of the street to the other in his sinuous route downhill.

"Where's your skateboard, Wally?" Marie asked.

"My mom was mad at me because I scraped myself up again."

"Everybody falls skateboarding. You have to expect it."

"My mom doesn't. Don't your folks worry about you getting hurt?"

Marie smiled wryly. "They don't worry about us."

"You're lucky."

"You think so? Yeah. Probably I'd hate it if I had the kind of mother who was on my back all the time." Marie shook her hair away from her face, and eyes gleaming boldly, said, "Leastways, I'm free to be me." Yes, Wally thought. She'd be the girl Jon-o would pick.

"You bringing me lunch, Wally?" Nick teased about the plastic bag.

"It's my lunch. Is it okay if I hang out with you guys today?"

"Sure. We'd even've fed you. So long as you eat peanut butter. We never run out of peanut butter. Bread maybe, but not the sticky stuff."

"I eat everything," Wally said.

"Like your brother. He ate whatever wasn't nailed down," Nick said.

"Last night I got so mad at Jon-o," Marie murmured. "I was waiting for him to call me and he didn't — I keep forgetting he's dead."

Nick turned incredulous blue eyes on his sister which didn't stop Wally from confiding eagerly, "Jon-o talks to me. Anyway, he *was* talking to me, but he must've got mad at me or something because he hasn't been around all week."

"You're both crazy. Ready for the loony bin. Nuts!" Nick said. "What do you mean, 'he hasn't been around,' Wally? We buried him weeks ago. I was there. You were, too."

"But I see him," Wally said. "And it's his voice."

"What does he say?" Marie asked quietly.

"Just about what's going on, how I should act, you know, regular stuff."

"Ask him sometime if he misses me," she said in a husky voice.

"That's it. I'm not listening to you weirdos. Whoo!" Nick strode off toward the house, swinging his heavy skateboard easily.

"I guess I *am* crazy," Wally said. "I mean I know I can't really — that Jon-o's not walking around talking to me still. But it seems so real that, like you said, I forget he's not alive."

"He was too full of life to die," Marie said. "I saw him when he jumped in the river after that kid. He didn't even take his hightops off. He heard the kid yell and took off. I saw him go over the falls with the kid's arm around his neck." She was clutching her fists to her chest, and she shook her head in disbelief. Then she let her breath out slowly and said, "I believe his spirit comes to you, Wally. I wish he'd come to me, too. I loved him." She turned abruptly toward the house.

Not sure what he should do, Wally took the peanut butter invitation to heart and trotted after them. He entered the house through the kitchen door. The Bowens' kitchen was grimy. Mom washed the enamel surfaces of her refrigerator, stove, and dishwasher often, but about the only thing in this kitchen that looked washed were the dishes standing in the drain rack to dry.

A plastic drum of peanut butter was on the table with a loaf of white bread open beside it. Wally liked white bread, but Mom bought whole grains. He made himself a peanut butter sandwich, and asked if anyone wanted to share his slightly squashed tuna fish.

"Your mom made it?" Nick asked. He was cutting himself a hunk of baloney which he'd taken from a refrigerator stocked mostly with beer.

"Aunt Flo did, I think."

"I like your mom's tuna fish," Nick said.

"Come over, and she'll give you the recipe anytime, Nick."

Nick nodded, but Wally didn't think he'd come, not without Jon-o being there. Nick wasn't outgoing like Jon-o, and he was more realistic. He was the one who'd deflate Jon-o's enthusiastic tall tales. "A dozen baskets in a row? More like four or five," Nick would say. And Jon-o would grin sheepishly and say, "Well, anyway that was some basketball game we played, wasn't it?"

"So how's the skateboarding coming now?" Nick asked.

"I'm getting the turns better," Wally replied.

"Think you want to be part of the exhibition?"

"You're having it?"

"Sure. We'll set up a slalom run to the ditch with some of those orange cones the road crews use. Jumping the ditch'll be the big event. Although I don't know who'd be impressed. Little kids maybe."

Wally immediately thought of Jon-o's tree and suggested that they charge admission and use the money to get a tree for Jon-o. Nick got interested when Wally explained that Jon-o's gravesite needed some shade and mentioned what the cemetery charged for a tree.

"That's a rip-off," Nick said. "Okay, we'll try charging. How much?"

"A dollar?"

"A dollar?" Nick questioned. "Come on, Wally, nobody's going to fork out a dollar to watch a bunch of kids show off."

"Yes, they will," Marie said. "We'll put flyers around

town advertising it. There's not much going on in the summer."

"And when are we going to do the show?"

"It better be when the garage is closed," Wally said.

"How about doing it next Sunday," Nick said.

"Who's going to do the notices?" Wally asked.

"I'll print one and make copies," Marie offered.

"And I'll stick them up in places where kids'll see them like on telephone poles near the park and bulletin boards in the supermarket," Wally offered eagerly. He would get his exercise walking this week.

"You coming to help steal the cones too?" Nick asked him slyly.

"Steal?" Wally questioned.

"I figured that word would get you." Nick's grin was mocking. He had tagged Wally as unnaturally law-abiding ever since the day Wally had tried to stop Jon-o from practicing driving Mom's car in the driveway. Wally had been scared because Jon-o didn't have a license.

"Wally's a stickler for permission slips," Jon-o had infuriated Wally by saying that afternoon.

"Permission slips are boring, Wally," Nick had said with amusement.

Now Nick relented and said, "We'll just borrow the cones and put them back after the exhibition."

"Okay," Wally said, "I'll help you."

"You sure you want to be part of this caper?" Nick's eyes mocked him again.

"Sure." Jon-o would do it. So would he. "When are you going to go?"

"How about tomorrow after lunch? They're repairing the highway near the new supermarket, and the road crews don't work on Sundays. Hal can drive us. He's got his license."

"Okay," Wally agreed. "I'll be here."

"I guess we're set then," Nick said, "and we didn't even have Jon-o to organize us."

He was getting there, Wally thought — one of the gang, cool. Now if he could only jump that ditch on the skateboard, Jon-o would be proud of him. He'd even be proud of himself. He walked home whistling, or trying to. Neither he nor his brother had ever been good at whistling.

"So now what, Jon-o?" Wally said. "It can't be the skateboarding you're mad about anymore." Unless it was action, not words that Jon-o was holding out for.

"Okay, okay, you'll see. And then you'll have to come back," Wally said.

A kid riding past on a bicycle looked at him strangely. He was talking out loud, Wally realized. He shut up and hurried on home.

Chapter 8

Wally only remembered he was supposed to be coming from the park with Nicole when he was face to face with Aunt Flo, who was working with Mom at the kitchen table. Mom was writing more notes to thank the people who had sent flowers or made donations to charities in Jon-o's memory. Aunt Flo was addressing the envelopes for her.

"There you are, darling," Mom said. "Did you have a good day?"

"Um hmm," Wally answered. He tensed for Aunt Flo to notice that Nicole wasn't with him.

"Wally, would you believe we've already received over a hundred cards?" Mom said, "And most of these names are new to me. Did you ever hear of a Stanley Remitz? He wrote a touching note about how Jon-o saved him from becoming a thief by lending him money at a crucial moment."

"Jon-o lent a lot of kids money," Wally said. He took a container of milk from the refrigerator.

"Where's Nicole?" Aunt Flo suddenly wanted to know.

"We got separated." Wally offered the half truth uneasily. "She isn't here yet?"

"Wally, you were supposed to stay together," Mom said.

"Well, she was in the rose garden, and I didn't want to hang around there." Another half truth that felt like a lie, was a lie really. He chewed on his lip and shifted from foot to foot.

"She's probably frantic looking for you, thinking you got kidnapped or something," Aunt Flo grumbled.

"I doubt it," Wally said. "Don't worry. She'll come home." The strain of not telling was bad, and he was relieved when Aunt Flo let up on him.

"It's four o'clock now; I'll give her till five," she said to her sister. "Then I'll borrow your car to look for her, Cyn."

"Of course," Mom said. "So what did you do with yourself all day, Wally?"

"Just walked around mostly."

"Oh, darling, guess what? Aaron called you." Mother looked pleased for him because Wally had confided that it bothered him that Aaron never thought to call him, even though they were friends. "He wanted to know if you could come over, and since you went to his house last, I invited him here for lunch tomorrow." She smiled expectantly.

Wally gulped. "You invited him here?" How was he going to go to Nick's for the cone caper with Aaron around? "I — uh, that's nice." He'd think of something.

Nicole walked in a minute under the deadline. "Wally, where were you?" Her tone made it sound as if he'd done something wrong.

"I guess we must've missed each other in the park."

"We sure did. I looked all over for you."

He frowned at her. Where did she get off putting him on the spot? "I was around."

"Well, I checked out all the playgrounds and didn't see you."

"Hey, Nicole!" he protested indignantly.

"It's too bad you two missed each other, but anyway, you're both home safe and sound now," Mom said to calm them.

Nicole yawned. "I'm pooped. I think I'll take a little nap."

"You do that, honey," Aunt Flo said. "Wally can set the table tonight."

He set it, growling under his breath at Nicole's sneakiness. She'd made him look bad when she was the one who'd been bad. Just let her ask him for another favor!

Just let her ask him to help her see her boyfriend tomorrow morning, for instance, and he'd tell her where to go. Meanwhile he had to figure out how he'd get to Nick's with Aaron here.

Sunday morning the rain was back, but the gray weather suited Wally's mood. At breakfast, Nicole said that she was going over to the mall, that she'd made a friend in the park yesterday and they'd agreed to shop together.

"Window shop, you mean," Aunt Flo said. "You've bought all the clothes you're getting for this summer, Nicole."

"Don't worry, I won't spend any money."

"What's she like, this friend you made in the park?" Aunt Flo asked.

"Well, she's tall and she has brown hair, and we hit it off right away. I don't know much about her yet, Ma. That's why we're meeting, to get to know each other."

"You're welcome to invite her here," Mom said.

"Maybe I will." Nicole even accepted the ride Mom offered, which Wally thought was pretty slimy of her since he would bet the tall, brown-haired friend she was going to meet was not a girl at all.

Aaron's parents dropped him off promptly at twelve. Mom and Aunt Flo fussed over the two of them, making them sandwiches to order — bacon, lettuce, and tomato for Aaron and the same with peanut butter for Wally.

"Gross," Aaron said when Wally started biting into his sandwich.

"It was one of his brother's favorite combinations," Mom explained.

"But it's really good," Wally said. "Taste it?"

Aunt Flo was the only one who took him up on his offer. She tasted, raised her eyebrows, and admitted, "Not bad."

After chocolate cookies and milk, Wally asked if it was okay if he and Aaron went for a walk. "There's something I want to show him."

"What?" Aaron asked.

"It's raining outside. What do you want to show him?" Mom asked also.

Wally gulped and thought fast. "Just something. If I describe it, it won't be a surprise."

"Is it animal, vegetable, or mineral?" Aaron promptly wanted to know. He liked quiz games.

"Animal." Wally knew that category would interest Aaron most. He was nutty about dogs. His mother said they weren't home enough to have one of their own, but Aaron would stop to pet even the dirtiest stray. Spot would have to do as the surprise. Wally suspected Aaron was not going to like the cone caper. Well, borrowing wasn't stealing, and if it didn't take too long, they could come back to the house and play.

"We'll be back soon," Wally said. "A couple of hours maybe."

"A couple of hours? Wally, where are you going?" Mom asked.

"Just to Jon-o's friend's house."

"But it's raining out," Mom repeated as if he hadn't understood her the first time.

"Just drizzling now," Aunt Flo said from behind the Sunday paper.

Mom badgered Wally about exactly where he was going, and when he mentioned the street address, she asked, "Isn't that where Nick lives?"

"Shush." Wally put his finger to his lips. "You'll give away the secret." Before she reacted to that one, he set off with Aaron in tow.

"So what kind of an animal?" Aaron asked as they sloshed through puddles.

"One you'll like, you'll see."

"If I guess right, will you tell me?"

Aaron was sharp. In nothing flat he'd guessed dog, so Wally leveled with him. "Look, Aaron, the deal is, I promised Jon-o's friend Nick to help him collect plastic cones to make a slalom run. We're going to have a skateboarding exhibition."

"A skateboarding exhibition? I didn't even know you knew how to skateboard."

"Yeah, I do, sort of."

"Well, how about teaching me."

"You want to learn?" An idea began to perk in Wally's brain.

"Maybe. I'd like to try it once, anyway."

"Would you be willing to pay a buck to try it, I mean with instructions from an expert?"

"You're an expert?"

"No, not me." Wally had Nick and Marie in mind.

"Sure, I'd pay a buck."

"Hmm," Wally said. "We could have lessons at the exhibition too. It's going to be kind of like stunt stuff — we're going to leap a ditch."

"*You're* leaping a ditch? On a skateboard?" Aaron's disbelief shook Wally's confidence. Could he really make himself do it?

"Maybe I am," Wally said. He straightened up and leaned forward to imitate Jon-o's ground-eating lope.

"Hey, hold up," Aaron complained. Short as he was, he had to run to keep pace with Wally.

The rain picked up speed as they reached Nick's house. It seemed to be trying to put out the flames painted around the hood of Hal's poison-green sedan which was pulling into the street with Nick inside it. Nick leaned back and opened the rear door for Wally. "You're just in time."

"Can my friend Aaron come too?" Wally asked.

Nick looked over at Hal who was driving. "What do you think?"

"Him and his friend can pick up the cones," Hal said.

"How about it, Wally? That okay with you?" Nick asked.

Wally was mystified. Why did they want him to pick up the cones? "Well, if they're not too heavy, I guess," he said.

They got into the backseat amid the discarded beer cans and fast-food wrappers. "So where's the amazing dog?" Aaron asked.

"Actually, it's just an ordinary dog," Wally confessed.

"So if it's ordinary, why'd you make such a big deal about it?"

"Because I told Nick I'd help him with the cones, and I didn't know if you'd come if I just asked you to."

"I don't like being tricked," Aaron said. He folded his arms across his narrow chest and wouldn't talk to Wally on the drive to the crosstown spur. There the highway department was resurfacing the fast lane next to the median guardrail. A long row of orange plastic cones guided cars to the stoplight at the intersection of the supermarket.

"How's it look?" Hal asked Nick.

"Nobody'll notice us in this rain," Nick said.

Hal pulled up inches from the metal guardrail and set his flasher. Nick got out of the car and said, "Okay, you kids stack up as many cones as'll fit in the trunk." Hal handed Nick the key to the trunk.

Wally climbed over Aaron and stepped out into the rain. "Come on, Aaron."

"No way. I'm not stealing anything." Aaron's face was grim above his folded arms.

"It's not stealing. We're just borrowing them. We're going to return them right after the exhibition."

"Uh uh," Aaron said with a stubborn shake of his small head.

Nick was watching from behind the open trunk lid. The rain had darkened his hair and slicked it down making him look tough. Wally asked him, "How come you're not helping pick them up?"

Nick groaned and admitted, "The thing is, they won't hassle a kid your age much if we get caught."

Wally stared at him. He had trusted Nick. Nick was Jon-o's best friend.

"Okay, okay," Nick said. "Stop looking at me that way. I'll do it." His long legs had him way down the line stacking cones before Wally took a step from the car. Nick swung back to the trunk with four cones as Wally began gathering up the two nearest ones. Cars swished past behind him. He didn't look for fear one of them would be flashing a light on top. If he got arrested, would they handcuff him? Did they put eleven year olds in jail cells? And how could he possibly make his mother understand why he'd done it?

"Since when do you borrow anything without permission?" was all she would have to ask him.

The plastic cones were heavier than he'd imagined. He shivered miserably in the warm rain as he brought his own two to the trunk. Nick fitted them in, left the trunk open, and got back into the passenger seat. Wally returned for the last two cones and wedged them into the trunk by himself. He slammed the lid down and scooted for the safety of the back seat, feeling vaguely criminal. But they weren't stealing anything, really — or were they?

Hal took off with a squeal of tires, shoving Wally back against his seat. Jon-o would have gotten a kick out of this caper. He'd be laughing up a storm, Wally told himself. But he wasn't Jon-o. Not yet. He was just his old overcautious self.

Hal did a U-turn around the median at the next light and was heading back up the other side of the highway when the red lights began flashing. "Oh oh," Nick said. "Trouble."

"Did I go through a light or something?" Hal asked nervously. He parked the car and rolled the window down for the short policeman who was already at the door, dry and official-looking in his gray rain gear.

"Let's see your license and registration."

"What'd we do, officer?" Hal asked.

The policeman didn't answer until he had Hal's license in his hands. Then he examined each of their faces. But his question was directed at Wally. "What did you take those road cones for?"

"We were just borrowing them," Wally said. "We're going to put them back."

"He did it on a dare," Aaron suddenly spoke up for him. "He was just proving that he wasn't scared. It's like an initiation, like college kids in a fraternity."

Wally and Nick and Hal looked at Aaron in surprise. The officer grunted. Then he took down all their names and addresses. "I'm going to have to call your parents," he told them.

"Please, don't do that," Wally begged. "We'll put the cones back right now."

"You sure will," the officer said, "but I'm still calling your parents."

Wally gulped.

.   .   .

"I told you," Aaron said on their way back to Nick's house after replacing the cones. "I told you you'd get in trouble."

"Shut up, you little creep," Hal snapped. Nick didn't say anything.

When they got out of the car, Aaron immediately started off for the long hike back to Wally's house where his parents were supposed to pick him up. He showed no interest in Spot who was on the front porch wagging his tail and barking for attention.

Without a word to Nick, Wally trudged after Aaron.

Nick was a disappointment. Wally had relied on him to protect him the way Jon-o would have, not to make him the fall guy. Mom would never understand when the policeman called to tell her her good little boy had been caught breaking the law. And Aaron's parents! Wow, Wally thought. They'd really be upset.

"How come you told that policeman it was for a fraternity initiation?" Wally asked Aaron when he caught up with him.

"To help you," Aaron said. "Fraternity guys don't get in much trouble if they get caught. My cousin's got a couple of street signs in his bedroom, and his parents don't even care."

"Thanks," Wally said. He didn't know if it had helped, but he was glad that Aaron still cared enough about him to try. "I'm sorry, Aaron. It wasn't a very fun afternoon."

"Well, it was an experience," Aaron said. "I'm still mad that you tricked me though."

"Yeah, I'll never do that again."

Aaron nodded. "You better not . . . Okay," he forgave Wally.

Whew! Wally let out breath he hadn't even realized he'd been holding in. Now all he had to worry about was parents, Aaron's two and his one. And where are you, Wally asked his brother silently. The least Jon-o could do was come and comfort him.

He dropped back behind Aaron. "Tell me it's no big

deal, Jon-o," Wally whispered to himself. "Tell me every-thing'll work out okay. Tell me something." That he hadn't seen Jon-o in a week made Wally feel worse than the fix he was in. And it was so unfair because he was doing the things Jon-o would have done, wasn't he? Even to getting in trouble.

Chapter 9

The phone call from the police came in the middle of Wally's favorite sitcom, which was too bad because Aunt Flo flicked off the TV and the grilling began. She and Mom stood side by side to back him into a corner of the couch with their whys and how-could-yous. Nicole sauntered through the living room, interrupting the rhythm of their twin hammer blows to ask, "He didn't shoot anybody, did he?"

"Nicole, you keep out of this," Aunt Flo said.

"Well, stealing junk like that doesn't exactly sound like he's headed for a life of crime. I mean, it's not like he robbed a liquor store or somebody's house."

"Is *that* what your father and I taught you?" Aunt Flo squealed. "There is *no* kind of stealing that's okay, Nicole."

"I wasn't stealing. I was borrowing the cones," Wally said for the fourth time. Nicole grunted in disgust and flounced off. He was sorry to lose her. Sneaky as she could be, at least she'd stood up for him.

"Wally," Mom said, "you *know* that taking something without permission is wrong." Her eyes were so clouded with grief that it hurt Wally to look at her.

"I'm sorry, Mom. I won't ever do it again."

"I don't understand what's gotten into you. You were such a good boy, but lately you're always in trouble. Why, Wally?"

"I guess — I don't know."

"He's following in his brother's footsteps. That's why," Aunt Flo said.

Mom turned on her sister angrily. "What do you mean? Are you insinuating that Jon-o wasn't good?"

"Listen, he was a remarkable boy, but he got into plenty of scrapes — mischief. You said yourself you couldn't control him, Cyn."

"I shouldn't have complained about Jon-o. I should have given him more credit for all he did right," Mom said, and she bit her trembling lip.

"Anyway —" Aunt Flo turned on Wally again. "Jon-o never stole anything, did he?"

Mother took a deep breath and realigned herself with Aunt Flo. "Wally, what will I do with you? Lately, you run out of here without letting us know where you're going. You do dangerous things like skateboarding. You promise to behave, but you don't. It seems I've got to punish you to convince you to take me seriously."

"You've upset your mother very much," Aunt Flo put in in case he'd missed the message.

Never in his life had he disappointed his mother this much. And remembering how angry he used to get at Jon-o for upsetting her, Wally felt bad, bad enough to welcome punishment. The worst she'd ever laid on Jon-o was no TV, or no allowance. Wally hoped it would be no TV because if she took away his allowance, that'd slow down Jon-o's tree fund.

"You're not to leave this house and yard for a week," Mom said, and Wally could practically hear her gavel smack the table. Even Aunt Flo looked impressed.

"A whole week?" Wally bleated.

"A whole week beginning right now."

He would have argued for a lighter sentence, but with Aunt Flo there to back Mom up, he knew he didn't have a chance. He slunk off to the den and opened the box with his bags of stamps and albums. But there wasn't anyplace he could spread them out to work on comfortably, and besides he didn't feel like it. Instead he got out the biography of the astronauts Aunt Flo had given him on his last birthday. This was the week to read it.

Early the next morning as Wally was eating his cereal, another blow fell. Aaron called and began ominously, "Guess what?"

"What?"

"That policeman called my parents just in case they

didn't know what I was doing yesterday afternoon. Now I can't see you anymore. My mom says you're a bad influence on me."

"But Aaron — for how long?"

"Forever maybe. Gee, Wally, I'm sorry. We should've stayed at your house; then — Hey, listen, I gotta go. The camp bus just honked. Bye."

Wally dumped the rest of his cereal. He'd lost his appetite.

It was a shimmering green summer day. He weeded the garden, checked for bugs, then tried to coax Nicole out of her lawn chair to play a board game with him. She shook her head and said she was busy thinking about Barney and didn't feel like playing childish games.

In the afternoon, he called Nick's house. Marie answered and said Nick had a job at the garage now. "I made twenty copies of the announcement," she told Wally. "You could start putting them up today."

"I can't. I'm not allowed out of the house this week because the police called here about those cones."

"No kidding! Your mother was that mad?"

"She thinks I'm getting wild."

Marie giggled.

"What's so funny?"

"If she thinks *you're* wild, she'd call us a bunch of outlaws," Marie said.

Wally thought that was likely. "So what did your folks say when the police phoned?"

"Not much. Dad just asked Nick when he was going to grow up."

What made being bad more serious for him, Wally guessed, was that he'd gotten Mom's expectations up too high by being good for so long. Weird that a history of good behavior could work against you.

"Look, don't worry about it," Marie said. "I can get plenty of kids to put up the posters, especially if I say it's for Jon-o."

"But what's Nick going to do about the slalom run? Use the tires?"

"No. It turns out Winston's got a friend who works in the highway department. In their garage. He'll lend us the cones."

"So we didn't even have to steal them?"

"Look, stop worrying and start practicing for the leap. See you Sunday, okay?"

"Okay." He hung up without mentioning that he couldn't very well practice since he was confined to his own yard.

By Wednesday, Wally had finished the biography about the astronauts and boxed the outgrown toys in the basement to give away. He considered vacuuming the old rug Jon-o had laid on top of the concrete floor down there, but he didn't feel like it. He used to spend a lot of time in the basement with army men and blocks, and before that with a tricycle that he rode around and around the edges of the rug, but the area seemed too dim and damp to him now. He dragged upstairs and Aunt Flo snagged him.

"Bored, Wally? How about organizing your mother's coupons? She's got a boxful here, but half of them are out of date."

"No, thanks."

"What do you mean, no? Don't you want to help your mother out?"

"Okay, okay." Wally set to work. At first, he didn't mind; he liked feeling useful. But Aunt Flo kept talking at him from the stove where she was concocting one of her economy casseroles from canned fish and fresh vegetables.

"While you're at it, you might as well separate the coupons into piles — soap and paper products in one, dairy in another — you know what dairy is? Cheese and milk and —"

"I know, Aunt Flo."

"Too bad I don't have mine here so you could do them, too."

"I probably won't even get through these."

"Why not? Don't be lazy. Think of all your mother does for you."

"I help her out."

"Says who? You were supposed to put the garbage out this morning, but you didn't, did you?"

"I forgot."

"How convenient, forgetting what you don't like to do."

"I've been good all week," he said resentfully.

"You've been moping around here with a sour puss. Even Nicole's more cheerful."

Nicole was still on a high from her weekend with Barney and pleased with herself for having gotten away with it. Wally ripped up outdated coupons with a vengeance, wishing Aunt Flo would stop bugging him. He was halfway through the pile when she plopped herself down in a chair across from him.

"Your mother should never have had boys," Aunt Flo said. "Even as a kid she was dainty and didn't like to get her hands dirty or play rough. *I* was the tomboy. I should have had the sons. . . . Believe you me, Wally, if you were my kid, you wouldn't be roaming around getting into trouble."

"I don't get in trouble," he snarled through clenched teeth.

"Don't you talk to me in that tone."

"Why do you always pick on me then?" Wally demanded.

"I don't pick on you. We're just having a conversation."

"Well, I hate your conversations," he yelled. Instantly, he regretted his outburst, but it was too late.

Aunt Flo reared back from the table and pointed a commanding finger at him. "You go to your room, and don't come out until supper."

He stomped up the stairs, forgetting that the den was

his room now. Nicole was lying on his old bed reading. "What's the matter with you?" she asked.

"I can't stand your mother."

"What'd she do to you?"

"Nag, nag, nag. She thinks I'm really bad, and I'm not."

Nicole snickered. "She thinks all boys are trouble." She smiled complacently. "Lucky for me I'm a girl."

Wally stomped back down to the den and shut the door behind him. He sat for an hour with his chin on his fists and his stomach churning, staring out the window. Nothing exciting ever happened on their quiet street. A taxi passed. A tiny lady walked by with a big hulk of a woolly white dog on a leash. "Look at that dog, Jon-o," Wally said, but Jon-o didn't materialize. Loneliness crept up on Wally and invaded every cell of his body.

It had been bad enough losing his brother without losing Jon-o's spirit, too. "It's not fair," Wally protested. "It's just not fair." Being good was the problem. Jon-o used to kid him about being so good. "You got to live a little, Wally," he'd say. "Loosen up and kick up your heels." How was he ever going to do that now without Jon-o to show him how? "I miss you so much," Wally said. Then he lay down on the daybed and squeezed his eyes shut against everything.

"Dinner, Wally," Aunt Flo said from the doorway.

"I'm not hungry."

"Your mother's home. Don't you want to say hi to her?"

"No."

"No? Well, suit yourself."

Next his mother walked into his room. "Why were you fresh to your aunt?"

"She nagged me."

"You have no right to be fresh to her."

"I hate her."

"Oh, Wally, please! She cooks and cleans and does everything she can to make my life easier. She's giving up her whole summer for me."

"You don't understand, Mom." He writhed in frustration at not being able to make her understand.

"I want you to come to the dinner table and eat, and I want you to apologize to your aunt. For my sake, Wally."

He went. He apologized stiffly. In return Aunt Flo and Mom gave him the silent treatment. Only Nicole would even look at him. She rolled her eyes and made funny faces, but it didn't help. Not being talked to bothered Wally more than he expected. Just to make them say something, he walked out of the kitchen without clearing the table. It was his turn, but they let him go without a word, and then he felt guilty about not doing his job.

He took a mystery book from Jon-o's library shelf and went to his room to read. He read the whole evening and no one came near him.

He fell asleep right away, but then he woke up. The house was still. The streetlights along with a full moon lit up the room. He rolled around trying to go back to sleep, but he couldn't. He was still furious with Aunt Flo and with Mom, too. It was hot. He was sweaty. He sighed a lot and wished he could smash something. Finally, without much thought, he got out of bed and dressed.

Once Jon-o had been out in the garage. Maybe that's where he was hanging out. If he wasn't, his skateboard would be, and Wally had an urge to touch it. He thought about the leap he wanted to make on Sunday at Nick's house. Leaping that ditch could mean a broken leg for him, or worse, a broken back. Maybe he'd be paralyzed for life, and Mom would have to take care of him. Rotten. He'd hate that. Being confined to a wheelchair. He couldn't even stand being confined to the house, much less a wheelchair. What he ought to do was practice more. But he wasn't allowed out of the yard and he wasn't allowed to use the skateboard. He wasn't allowed anything. They wanted him to be a mama's boy, useless as a ball of dried out Play-Doh. Well, he wouldn't go along with it.

He slipped out of the house and eased the garage door up. They had better all be sleeping soundly.

The skateboard had a satisfying heft and a slick feel except where Jon-o had put sandpaper tape on the top. Wally spun the wheels and imagined himself sailing along, his arms held just so. He'd bend his knees, and then he'd soar over the ditch, with the board glued to his feet by momentum, and land perfectly on the blacktop pad his brother had designed. Jon-o would appear and he'd applaud. "Way to go, little brother. Way to go!"

With the skateboard gripped under one arm and without making a conscious decision, Wally started walking toward the cemetery. He didn't feel Jon-o's presence, not in the garage, not anywhere. Maybe Jon-o was finished with being alive and had settled into being a dead body in his grave. Not likely. Not Jon-o. He'd never been still for very long at a time.

Wally felt strange hearing his own footsteps in the quiet, passing from the lighted orbit of one streetlamp to the pale orbit of the next. He felt as if he were walking in a dream, protected from whatever was in the dark around him. Cars swished by, but he didn't look at them. He didn't even sneak glimpses of other people's lives through their lighted windows. Walking felt good. Slowly, the storm of anger and despair inside him quieted.

What could Mom do to him for running out in the middle of the night? Send him to reform school? Wally doubted it. Unless Aunt Flo made her. Without Aunt Flo around, Mom would be so easy to get along with. "You're her favorite," Jon-o used to accuse him. But he wasn't, Wally knew. He was just the baby. Jon-o was the favorite, the one who lit up Mom's life.

It was a long walk to the cemetery, and once there,

Wally thought maybe his need for adventure had been satisfied. He stood outside looking at the moon-silvered tombstones. The somber stones had a presence they didn't have by day. They seemed to be doing sentry duty for their dead.

The cemetery was deserted. To get to Jon-o's grave, Wally would have to walk the road where he'd seen the gardeners. Scary, he thought, to be wandering in that place alone at night. Suppose he got lost and couldn't find Jon-o's plot. What if he couldn't find his way out? He might die of fright, have a heart attack maybe. So go home if you're scared, he told himself. He shifted the heavy skateboard to his other arm. What if he made himself take just one run down the hill and see if he could turn? Did he dare? Jon-o would have. Jon-o wouldn't have let himself be spooked.

Wally started off rapidly past the entrance pillars and to the right. His heart was beating as fast as his feet were moving, faster. Scared. He was scared. Though the moon lit the roadway before him, the light was eerie. Without allowing himself time to think, he climbed the hill, set down the skateboard, and shoved off.

For the first time, his body felt fluid, and instead of worrying about falling, he concentrated on controlling the board, pressing to one side and then the other with his knees. The board yielded to his will easily. At the bottom of the hill, he did a neat reverse and snapped up the board. Not bad, he told himself. Exhilarated, he climbed back up and tried again. The third ride was smoothest of all. Now he could do it. It felt easy. Maybe he needed some more practice, but basically, he had mastered it.

Tree branches whispered and the light flickered. "Jon-o," Wally called softly. "You there?" He resisted the temptation to cut and run. Marie had come at night and not been afraid. If there were any ghosts about, they weren't going to bother him. What did they care about Jon-o's little brother? Still, Wally was nervous leaving the hill to make the last turn in the dark toward where Jon-o had been buried, and he was glad when he arrived to find the new grave so brightly spotlighted that if there had been a marker to read, he could have read it.

"Hey, Jon-o, I'm here," Wally said. "And this is your skateboard." Something chirruped and a bird flew across the face of the moon. Not a bird, Wally thought, a bat probably since it was nighttime. "I hope you're not still mad at me," Wally said. "I'm trying, Jon-o. I'm really trying. . . . Why can't you talk to me anymore? What are you doing anyway? Is there time when you're dead? I mean is it like stopped, or does it keep going? Is it boring? . . . If there's rules, you've probably already figured how to get around them. . . . I wish you'd go back to talking to me, Jon-o. I wish you were alive to talk to me. You had no right to die and leave me without anyone to tell me things."

Wally let out an angry wail from the depth of his frustration. He wailed and yelled until he'd emptied himself out. Then he hurried back the way he'd come, suddenly anxious to leave the cemetery. He was in such a tearing hurry in fact, that he set the skateboard at the top of the last hill and rode it down. But the moon had moved, and it was dark at the bottom, and he fell.

He wasn't hurt. He picked himself up and ran out between the stone pillars.

And there was Jon-o waiting for him, tall and muscular, his eyes twinkling. "Not bad, little brother," he said and put his arm around Wally's shoulder. Wally could almost feel the warmth. His heart lifted. It felt so good.

"Where've you *been*?" Wally demanded.

"I've been around."

"I didn't see you."

"Could be you needed to get through some stuff on your own, Wally."

Wally thought about it as they walked toward home side by side. Maybe the week had been good for him in a way. Miserable as he had been, he did feel stronger now. "Well, but I like being with you, Jon-o."

"Listen," Jon-o said, "I didn't want to die. You keep acting like I did it on purpose. I didn't. It just happened to me."

"I know, but . . . you were going to take me camping with you someday," Wally said. Tears stung his eyes so he could barely see the street.

"Yeah. Well, you can still go. Join the Boy Scouts. They'll take you camping."

"But I wanted to go with you, Jon-o."

"You always wanted to go with me. It used to make me mad the way you hung on me. Didn't I tell you you had to do things on your own?"

"I'm trying."

"Yeah, you are."

"About that ditch, though," Wally said. "I'm not sure I can jump it. Would you help me maybe?" He looked around but Jon-o had disappeared.

Sighing, Wally walked the few remaining blocks home. He put the skateboard back in the garage, closed the front door behind him as quietly as he could, and sneaked into his room. Well, at least he'd practiced some. When the time came to do the leap, he wouldn't be entirely unprepared.

Chapter 10

Wally took it as a good sign that his week long confinement ended on the day of the skateboarding exhibition. While Aunt Flo concentrated on serving them her perfect golden pancakes, he explained to his mother why he had to be at Nick's. "See, the exhibition's to raise money for Jon-o's tree and I have to help."

"You're not going to be in the exhibition, are you? How are you going to help?" Mom asked with mild suspicion.

"Oh, you know, with tickets and whatever Nick says."

Mom gave him a loving smile over her coffee mug. "Sounds like fun. I hope you make a lot of money."

"I sure hope so. It was my idea to sell the tickets."

"What goes on in a skateboarding exhibition?" Aunt Flo asked.

"Well, tricks like wheelies and handstands and kick-turns and — Nick and Marie are good, like Jon-o was.

And I'm bringing Jon-o's skateboard for kids who want lessons," Wally added so that he wouldn't have to sneak it out of the garage.

Without warning, tears began flowing from his mother's eyes. Aunt Flo took her sister into her arms. They all knew by now how it was to have the ground give way and fall headfirst into grief.

Nicole hadn't seen anything. She was at the refrigerator getting herself a glass of milk. "I read a poster on a telephone pole about that skateboarding thing, but I didn't know it had to do with Jon-o," she said. "I'll come too."

"You're interested in skateboarding?" Wally was surprised.

"Well, I'd like to try it if the lessons don't cost much."

"Good," Wally said. "They're just a dollar."

His mother had control of herself by the time Nicole turned around.

"Neither you nor Wally should be skateboarding. Skateboards are dangerous," Aunt Flo warned Nicole. "I read an article by a doctor about what a menace they are."

"Not if you're careful, Aunt Flo," Wally said.

"Is that so! But you've been careful, haven't you? And you've hurt yourself *twice* on a skateboard already.

"That's true," Mom admitted. She frowned uncertainly.

Desperation inspired Wally. "Mom, when babies learn to walk, they fall down and get hurt sometimes, don't they? You wouldn't keep a baby from learning to walk because it might fall down, right?"

Mom began nodding, but Aunt Flo was fast to point out that walking was essential, and skateboards were not.

"Oh, Ma, don't be such a grouch," Nicole said. "When was the last time I fell down and hurt myself? When I was two or three?"

An hour later, Wally set off jubilantly with the skateboard, a bagful of safety pads, an old football helmet, and Nicole. The safety items and Nicole were camouflage. He didn't plan to let them get in the way of his big challenge today. "Nicole," he said as they crossed the main street at the light, "I never told about you and Barney, did I? Well, today you've got to keep what I do a secret. Okay?"

"What're you going to do?"

"Just something for Jon-o."

"Like what? What're you planning, Wally?"

"It's no big deal. I'm just going to leap a ditch on a skateboard."

Nicole stopped short in the middle of the road. When a car honked at her in warning, Wally took her arm and pulled her to the sidewalk. "I'm not going with you if you're set on killing yourself," she said. "I'm not going to be the one to give Aunt Cynthia more bad news. Besides, they'll say I should have stopped you because I'm older."

"Aw, come on, Nicole. It's not that dangerous."

"I don't know." Nicole didn't budge. "You're different since your brother died. I don't know what to expect from you."

Wally grinned, glad to hear it. It helped him to believe that he had changed enough to fly across the ditch, that he could be like his brother — at least for one daring act.

"What're you smiling about?" Nicole asked when Wally remained silent.

He shrugged and didn't answer. His silence must have had more effect on her than words because she finally said grudgingly, "Well, all right. I'll watch, but if anything bad happens, I'm telling on you, Wally."

Spot barked wildly at them from the open wooden porch of the Bowen house. Nicole stayed back even though the dog wriggled with delight the instant Wally began petting him. Nicole mistrusted animals the way Wally's mom did.

Bitsy opened the door to Wally's knock. She was sniffling. "I've got a cold," she said.

"That's too bad," he said. "Where's your brother and sister?"

"In the kitchen." Bitsy left the door open for him and returned to her nest of blankets in front of the TV.

Nicole looked warily about as she followed Wally

through the living room to the kitchen. As usual the Bowen parents were out and the house looked dingy. Nicole hung back without saying a word when Wally introduced her to Nick and to Marie, who was lifting delicious-smelling cookies off a sheet with a spatula.

Nick was preparing a packaged drink mix in a picnic jug. "Marie thinks we can sell this stuff," he said. "You want to be in charge of it, Wally?"

"I'm going to be in the exhibition," Wally reminded him.

"You been practicing?"

"Yes."

"You think you can jump that ditch?"

"Ummm."

Nick raised an eyebrow and squinted at Wally doubtfully, but all he asked was, "So what do you think about charging a quarter for a cookie and a drink?"

"It's just a four-ounce cup and a small peanut butter cookie," Marie said. "But it's for a good cause."

"If you have plastic wrap and ribbon," Nicole put in suddenly, "you could wrap the cookies fancy and charge more. That's what we did at a bake sale back home and we made a mint."

"Okay, Wally's cousin, you be in charge of refreshments," Nick said. "And if anyone wants lessons, Wally can handle it. He's got the patience. Me, I'll play policeman." Nick grinned.

"We're going to need a policeman if Hal and Winston bring those kids from the projects," Marie said.

"Want to see the landing pad, Wally?" Nick asked.

"Sure." Wally followed Nick out the back door, walking tall because Nick seemed to be treating him like an equal. It was only when they stood in the black-topped bowl and looked back across the ditch to the hill that a drum began to bang anxiously behind Wally's ribs.

A slalom course had already been laid out with Hal's orange plastic cones. It ended in a straight shot at the ditch which ran the length of the Bowens' property. The ditch was littered with junk now — plastic toys, dented soda cans, a couple of tires, soggy paper scraps. Was he really going to try and leap that four-foot-span? It didn't even seem possible. Wally swallowed dryly.

"Why don't you give it a try before everybody gets here," Nick said.

"Could you show me how you do it first?"

"Sure. Lend me Jon-o's board."

Wally had gotten so used to carrying the board, he'd forgotten it was still under his arm. While he was at it, he got rid of the bag of safety equipment by dropping it next to the landing pad.

Casually, the way Nick did everything, he ambled across a bridge of loose boards spanning the ditch, and climbed the slope. Seconds later, he was heading down on the skateboard, cranking his body as he expertly swung around the cones. He came off the last turn fast, crouched low and soared over the ditch. On the landing pad, he jumped to one side. The skateboard flipped up in the air and dropped onto the scanty grass of the yard. "Your turn," Nick said and handed Wally the board.

"No. I'm just going to do it once," Wally said, reasoning that he couldn't expect a miracle twice.

"Help us with this kitchen table, Nick," Marie called from the house. "Hurry." She and Nicole had gotten the chrome-legged table stuck in the doorway.

Nick strode to the rescue. He flipped the table sideways and angled it through the opening while the girls supported the back legs. "This is our refreshment stand," Marie said to Wally. She helped her brother walk the table over the board bridge and set it up in the garage's paved lot.

Nick said, "Listen, Wally, you better take a practice run if you really want to do this jump. And don't forget to get set back on the skateboard when you take off, or it'll pitch right into the ditch. I banged up my shins the first time I tried it."

"Thanks," Wally said. "I'll be fine." He wasn't worried. Jon-o would show up in time and be with him all the way. He wouldn't let his little brother down. "When are kids supposed to get here?"

"Soon. Are you scared? It's okay if you're scared. Jon-o used to say fear was the zinger that makes you outdo yourself." Nick looked at Wally hard. "All right, then try the slalom run at least so I can see how you're coming along." It was Nick's turf which gave him the right to give orders. He folded his arms to wait.

"Okay," Wally said coolly. He felt as cool as he'd sounded, too, until he reached the top of the slalom run at the level end of the parking lot near where the wrecker was parked. Then he made the mistake of looking down toward the ditch, and his cool iced over. The run was impossible. The turns were too sharp — left, right, left, straighten out, and over the ditch.

"Wait, and I'll move a couple of cones so you come off parallel to the ditch on your first try," Nick said.

Wally's knees went weak. He watched Nick rearranging the cones. He watched Marie and Nicole wrapping cookies and taping up prices on the refreshment table. He saw Bitsy snatch a couple of cookies when their backs were turned. He noted that she held a pink woolly rag around her shoulders. It seemed the only thing working in his body was his eyes.

"Okay, Wally." Nick stepped aside and waved Wally on.

Wally took a deep breath. "Jon-o. Hey, Jon-o, no way I can do this without you." Where was his brother anyway? Wally got angry. "Come on, this is for you. Help me!"

Nick was waiting. "Remember to lean into the turns, and don't forget to bend your knees," he called.

"Okay for you, Jon-o," Wally whispered to himself.

"Then I'll make it on my own." He took a deep breath, set his foot slantways on the skateboard, and pushed off. The first turn was a little awkward and he wobbled, but he made it and bent his knees and pushed his body more into the turn going around the second orange cone. He was doing it. He was doing it. But then there was another cone. It went over. Now he was angling toward the ditch instead of parallel to it. Going to crash. He was going to crash! In a panic, he twisted his body and lost his balance.

Nick got to him first, "You okay?"

"Yeah. What'd I do wrong?"

Nick helped him to his feet. "Everything. You still in one piece?"

"I guess so."

"You're lucky. You're not ready for the ditch, Wally."

Just then four boys arrived on bicycles. They hung back shyly next to the wrecker. Winston appeared, leading a miniparade of small children who were skipping and laughing and chasing each other. "You start doing wheelies yet?" he called out.

"We're waiting for you to show us how, Winston," Nick said. He left Wally and walked over to the wrecker.

Wally stood rubbing his finger over the sandpaper strips on the top of Jon-o's board. Nick didn't want him to jump that ditch. But he had to. He wasn't going to go back on his solemn promise and give Jon-o an excuse for not coming alive again.

"Hey, kid," a plump-cheeked boy of about nine with a skateboard under his arm said to Wally. "Is this where to get lessons?"

"Lessons?"

"On the skateboard." The kid tapped the board in Wally's hand. "They told me you're the teacher."

"Oh, yeah."

"How much," the kid said. "I hope it's not more than a dollar because that's all I've got."

"That's enough," Wally said.

"My name's Pete." Eager-eyed and trusting, the boy looked at Wally. He held out a clumsy-looking wooden skateboard. "My uncle gave me this for my birthday, but I keep falling off." When Wally didn't move, Pete dug his dollar out of his pocket and handed it over. Wally sighed deeply and got down to business.

"It's easier to get started on a little slope," he said. He could remember clearly how Jon-o had taught him. "Here, put your left foot near the front, a little sideways to the nose and push off with your right foot." He illustrated on Jon-o's board. "If you want to turn, you move your shoulders around the way you want to go, and then your feet kind of naturally follow." Doing it as he spoke, he made a smooth turn and an uphill stop. "Try it," he told the kid.

The boy put his left foot on his own skateboard, but it began to roll out from under him before he could get his right foot on it. "Try hanging onto my arm," Wally said, full of sympathy as his own awkward beginnings came back to him.

The wrecker was covered with kids climbing all over it. "When's the exhibition going to start?" one of them demanded loudly.

"Soon," Nick told him. He yelled for Marie to get her skateboard. Kids, mostly younger than Wally, were milling around like chickens in a barnyard now. Two of them started chasing each other around the slalom course.

"How am I doing?" Pete asked anxiously.

"Good," Wally said. "Bend your knees, like you're going to sit down. Don't stick your butt out." Slowly, Wally's self-confidence began to return.

He concentrated on getting Pete comfortable pushing off and turning, and when the plump-cheeked boy yelled, "Hey, I did it. I really did it," Wally felt good.

"Yeah, but how do you stop fast like if a car's coming," a boy with a floppy lock of dark hair and a sharp nose asked. He was standing anxiously at Wally's elbow.

Wally turned to answer and noticed a line of would-be students waiting for his attention. "You can jump off," Wally said, and demonstrated.

He told Pete to practice and asked, "Who wants to try it next?" The dollars slowly accumulated in his pocket. He sweated and concentrated on watching to see where his students were making their mistakes. "Don't be afraid of falling. Just relax and roll if you do," he told them.

Some kids had to be steadied as they balanced and a couple had to be picked up when they fell.

All the while questions and comments came shooting at Wally from every direction. "How come you've only got one board to use?" . . . "What makes you the teacher?" . . . "Why do we have to wait so long?"

Part of Wally's mind was aware that Nick was now weaving an invisible thread of motion around clusters of kids. His body loose and easy, Nick was a moving exhibit of how it would be when you had control of your board. He did a 180-degree kick turn and then when some boy asked him if he knew how to do a headstand, Nick did a perfect headstand.

"Can you do that?" Pete asked Wally.

"No." Pete looked so disappointed that Wally blurted out, "I can jump the ditch, though."

"Yeah?" Pete looked impressed. "When?"

"When we do the exhibition."

Awhile later Wally looked up from a pigtailed girl who had just managed a neater stop under his direction than he'd ever done himself. There was Nicole manning the kitchen table food stand alone, and sailing through the slalom course was Marie, sleek as a needle except that her joints seemed free to rotate in any direction. She came off the last turn leaning sharply, straightened, and flew over the ditch to a smooth landing. A spontaneous cheer went up from the kids who were crowding the sides of the slalom course. The exhibition was underway.

"Wow," Pete said. "She's good. Can you really do that?"

"I don't know," Wally mumbled. He watched Nick come down the slope and clear the ditch on his skateboard. Marie did a headstand and then a handstand. Kids clapped. They were more orderly now. Winston was clowning on Nick's skateboard.

"Your turn?" Wally's prize student asked.

"Yeah," Wally said. "It's my turn."

He grabbed Jon-o's skateboard away from a boy who hadn't even paid and was trying to use it. Then he squeezed through the kids crowding the slalom track and climbed to the top. He saw Bitsy, down near the ditch, slug a kid who tried to pull her woolly rag away from her. For a few seconds everything got quiet. Wally looked past the plastic cones to the ditch and couldn't imagine how his feet would stay on the board going over.

Nicole spotted him and screamed, "Wally, don't do it! You'll hurt yourself." She stood on tiptoe, clasping her hands.

"Come here, Wally. I got something to tell you," Nick's voice rang out like a concerned parent.

Kids started laughing. "Do it," some shouted.

"Go, Wally. Go!" Pete yelled encouragingly.

"Do it, do it, do it," the chorus chanted.

Nick and Marie were pushing through the crowd toward him. Wally got his foot set on the skateboard.

Whatever happened, he had to try. "Jon-o," he whispered. "I'm doing it. See?" and without waiting for Jon-o to appear, he pushed off.

He made it around the first cone and through the narrow gap Nick had set up between the next two, but he was going too fast. To the right, to the left. He tried to bend his knees and lean into the turns, but the crowd loomed close, and he was going too fast, and panic overtook him. He faltered and fell. He heard a scream, and felt a strange softness. He'd fallen onto someone. Someone else yanked him to his feet.

"Bitsy, you all right?" It was Nick, not anxious about Wally now, but about Bitsy who was lying on the ground, screaming.

"I thought you killed her," Pete said in awe.

"Bitsy, can you stand up?" Marie asked the child.

Bitsy reached up her arms, still howling, and Nick scooped her up. "Okay," he said. "The exhibition's over. That's it for today." He strode to his house with his sister in his arms.

"I'm sorry," Wally said. "Gee, I'm sorry."

"Go on home everybody," Marie said.

"You're not very good are you?" Pete asked Wally.

"He don't know how to skateboard," the pigtailed girl said. "I could do better than him."

"Some teacher! We ought to get our money back," another boy said.

"He was okay at teaching," Pete defended him.

Nicole grabbed Wally's arm. "Let's go. Come on, Wally."

Shame immobilized him. Finally, he bent down and picked up Jon-o's skateboard, not meeting anybody's eyes. Then Wally let his cousin lead him off the lot. He wished he had Bitsy's blanket to cover his head with. He wished he could hide in Jon-o's grave.

"You don't have to worry, I won't say a word to your mother," Nicole said.

It didn't matter anymore, Wally thought. Nothing worse could happen to him. He'd not only failed to jump the ditch, he'd injured a little girl. Jon-o was a hero, but Jon-o's little brother was a klutz and a clown. Now he'd done it. Now he'd lost his brother for sure.

Chapter 11

When he got home, Wally shut himself into the den and curled up on the bed. He didn't think about anything, just lay still with the defeat throbbing like an infected thumb. Footsteps, the sound of voices, the clink and clatter of dinner preparation, nothing roused him.

Finally, Nicole came to his door. "Wally, your mom wants to know what's the matter with you. I said you got upset about something at Nick's house and I didn't know what. I'm not going to tell them. I promise."

"It doesn't matter."

"Well, you have to get up for dinner."

"I'm not hungry."

"Don't you want to call and find out what happened to that kid you banged into?"

He sat up. "Would you call please, Nicole?" Wally was flooded with guilt suddenly, a double dose, first for hurting Bitsy and second for not even worrying about what had happened to her. "Nick's number's in Mom's telephone book."

"Okay, I'll call, but you better get up," Nicole said.

He sat without moving, his brain on hold until she returned.

"Marie said the kid was just scared. Nothing's broken or anything. Marie says they made a lot of money, and she wants to know how much you took in from the teaching."

Wally emptied his pockets of eleven dollars in bills and change. "I'm going to put in all the money I have in my bank besides," he said.

"Marie says she'll put in her baby-sitting money and Nick's contributing too," Nicole said. "I bet our mothers would help with the rest, seeing as it's for Jon-o. Marie wants to know if you're going to have some kind of tree planting ceremony."

Wally nodded. "Yeah, we should."

"Well? Aren't you glad it worked out?"

"I promised Jon-o I'd do the jump."

"Big deal. You were good at teaching those little kids, Wally. I watched you. Jon-o was good with little kids, too. Wasn't he?"

"But I couldn't make that jump."

"You're crazy," Nicole said. "You know you're really crazy? Your brother wouldn't want you to kill yourself."

"He wanted me to be special like he was."

"Everybody's special. You are too — just not on a skateboard."

He had failed, Wally thought. He had tried to measure up, but somehow at the last minute he had lost his nerve and turned the wrong way and knocked Bitsy down. He had been so sure he could do it, that he would sail like Jon-o, over that ditch — flying, the way Marie and Nick had flown. But he wasn't a flyer. He couldn't wear his brother's shining spirit even for a little minute. A good boy, his mother called him. That was all he was, a plain, ordinary, good boy.

. . .

They kept watching him as the week passed — Mom and Aunt Flo and Nicole. Wally could feel their eyes on him while he ate his meals and took out the garbage and worked in the garden.

The Tuesday after the skateboarding exhibition he got a phone call from Aaron.

"I'm home sick," Aaron said. "What are you doing?"

"Not much. How come you're calling me, Aaron?"

"Oh, it's okay. We can be friends again. Your mom called mine and explained how you're all worked up about your brother's death, so you're not acting normal. So now my mom says it's okay to see you as long as you come over here. How about Saturday?"

"I don't know," Wally said. "I'll call you."

He didn't feel like seeing Aaron. He didn't feel like doing much of anything. The first lettuce heads were shaping up. He watched the tender green leaves for bugs and pulled every weed in the garden as soon as it was big enough to get a thumb and finger on. The tomato plants were thriving too. Their coarse, lacy leaves spiked the air with an aromatic odor as he walked barefoot in the yielding soil. He spent a lot of time in the garden. Once a yellow butterfly landed on his arm and Wally wanted to call his brother to witness. It hurt to think that Jon-o wasn't around, wouldn't come around anymore now that Wally had failed him.

Wednesday night he gave up watching TV and went to bed early. He couldn't sleep and lay there staring at the ceiling. He'd been doing a lot of staring lately. He lacked the energy for anything that took more effort.

Presently the door opened and his mother came in. She sat down on his bed. Fair as she was, she seemed to glow in the dim late evening light. "You're wide awake, aren't you?" she said.

"Yeah."

"I want you to tell me why you're so depressed."

"I'm not depressed."

"Wally, it's important that you talk to me. You used to talk to me. When you were little, you trusted me with all your secrets. Remember?"

"I was a baby, Mom."

"You even told me once I was your best girlfriend."

"You still are. You're my only girlfriend. Girls don't like me."

"Don't worry, they will." She ran her cool hand over his forehead and through his hair. "Nicole says it has to do with what happened at Nick's house on Sunday," Mom said unexpectedly.

"No, it doesn't. It's — nothing's wrong with me."

"Tell me what happened Sunday . . . please, Wally."

"Nothing . . . I promised Jon-o I'd do something for him and then I couldn't do it."

"Why not?"

"Well," he said, "it was something you wouldn't have wanted me to do anyway."

"What? What was it?"

"Just something . . . Jon-o could have done it easy, and you'd never have known. But if I'd kept trying, I'd probably have hurt myself bad."

"I'm glad you didn't do it then."

"I meant to do it. I wasn't scared that much, but I just couldn't."

He probed the mystery. Why hadn't he done it? He had meant to; he'd been determined. What had made him jerk away from that straight shot at the ditch and run into Bitsy? He *must* have been scared; terrified of crashing and hurting himself.

"Do you think your brother would have wanted you to do something dangerous?"

"Well, but he didn't want me to be a mama's boy."

"You're not a mama's boy."

"Yeah, I am."

"If you mean you're careful and don't take foolish risks, then I'm glad you are."

"Jon-o was a hero, Mom. I'll never be a hero. I wish I'd died instead of him."

"No, Wally, no!" she cried. "You mustn't think that. You're different from your brother, but every bit as wonderful."

She was saying that to make him feel better, of course. It wasn't true, but he said, "Thanks, Mom. I think you're wonderful too."

She kissed him. "Wally," she whispered in his ear, and her tears tickled his face, "your brother loved you very much, not because you're like him, but because you're you. Don't try to be Jon-o. Be yourself. Be the good, deep, thoughtful boy you are."

She sat upright and turned as if she might go. Then she looked at him over one shoulder and murmured, "You know, when your father died, I didn't want to believe it, and I tried to keep him alive every way I could. Your aunt thought I should get rid of everything that reminded me of him, but I hid some of his clothes. Sometimes I'd sneak into the closet to smell them, and I — I imagined that he was talking to me."

She took Wally's hand in her own and said absentmindedly, "You have your father's hands, his long capable fingers. . . . It's hard, Wally. It's so hard to lose someone you love. It hurts so much that you try to protect yourself by — well, like you did by promising you'd do something impossible for Jon-o." She looked into Wally's eyes. "What I finally realized was, I didn't have to hold on to your father through all the photographs and letters and clothes he'd left behind. I had him in my heart. I have Jon-o there, too, and so do you."

"But I want him to be alive, Mom, really alive."

"Nothing stays alive forever. You know that — not even the earth, not even the stars. We all die sooner or later."

"But my brother's life was too short."

She pulled away and blew her nose. "Yes, it was." She sounded exhausted. "Anyway, I'm glad you're alive, darling, because I need you more than ever now."

He thought about it when she left, about how she needed him. It wasn't just a matter of mowing the lawn and remembering her birthday and Mother's Day. When she was tired or sad or sick, he'd be the one she'd have to turn to. He'd be the one to make her smile the way Jon-o used to sometimes. And the one to make her proud, the only one.

Well, he could do that. If he became a teacher maybe, or a doctor like Jon-o had wanted to be, then Mom would be proud of him. Jon-o would be too. It only took determination, which was one thing Wally knew he had.

· · ·

The tree dedication ceremony wasn't very big. The man at the cemetery had said it wasn't usual to have one, and Mom had promised there'd be just a few people and no fuss to speak of. Nick and Marie were there, dressed up the way they'd been for the funeral. Nicole and Aunt Flo stood beside Mom, and Wally stood on her other side, nearest the head of the grave where the stone would be laid when it was ready.

The gardeners had dug a big hole for the tree, but it was farther away than Wally thought was right. He got his mother to ask the nice gardener about it, the thin one, and the man said the hole was spaced correctly for the pine they had bought. It would shade the plot, as they wanted, when it grew up and spread out in a few years.

Wally and the others stood watching the two men plant the pine, which looked just like a Christmas tree. But it should have been bigger for what it cost, Wally thought. When the gardeners finished, they stepped back. The nice one rested on his shovel and looked to the family. "That's it then," he said. His partner picked up their tools and clattered them into the back of the truck. The nice one nodded at Wally and the others and opened his mouth to speak. He cleared his throat and nodded again. "Well, that's it," he repeated, and joined his partner in the truck. After the two had gone, everybody shifted about awkwardly.

Mom turned and asked, "Do you want to say something, Wally?"

He'd thought of a lot of things he could say, but standing there he was at a loss as to how to begin. It was hot with the sun aiming its rays at them through pure blue sky. Everyone was perspiring. Aunt Flo kept wiping her red face with tissues; she looked really uncomfortable. So Wally started. He spoke to his brother. "We got the tree for you, Jon-o. It's not a maple, but I hope you like it."

"Rest easy," Nick said as soon as Wally stopped talking. "We won't forget you."

"I love you, Jon-o," Marie whispered.

Nicole burst into tears, and Aunt Flo clasped her to her bosom and shook her head to indicate she didn't want to say anything. Her eyes were shiny with tears, too.

"I hope this tree grows as tall and beautiful as you were, son," Mom said quietly.

Everybody stood there for a minute, not sure if the ceremony was over or what to do next. Finally Aunt Flo said, "Well —" and she started to walk away, pulling Nicole along with her.

Mom turned to Nick and Marie and said, "Please. Come by and see us sometimes. You were Jon-o's closest friends and we don't want to lose you."

Nick nodded and mumbled something. Marie touched Mom's cheek with a kiss and the two Bowens left together.

"Coming, Wally?" Mom asked.

Wally nodded but he didn't budge as she turned to go. He looked at the grave and at the tree and wondered where Jon-o was. Did he know about the tree? Did it please him? A spasm of longing hit Wally. He missed his brother. Oh, how he missed him!

One foot after the other, Wally plodded down the hill to where his mother sat on a bench in the shade of a big tree. She looked so sad that he sat down next to her and hugged her. She shuddered.

"Mom," Wally said, "it'll be all right. . . . I love you, Mom."

"I can't bear it that he's gone," she whispered.

"But he's not, Mom. He's somewhere still. Don't you feel him?"

"Oh, Wally, you're so dear. You're strong and steady and sweet. I'm grateful to still have you."

"Cynthia?" Aunt Flo yelled from somewhere in the distance. "Are you coming?"

"Coming," Mom raised her voice to call. She stood up and swayed so that Wally reached out to keep her from falling.

He was holding her and facing the hill they'd just descended when he saw Jon-o. There he came, skateboarding down the hill, his long muscular body twisting gracefully through the turns and a grin on his face as big as life. "Mom, it's Jon-o," Wally cried gladly. "See him?"

She looked, but shook her head. Too blinded by tears and weak with grief to see anything, she leaned on Wally's shoulder.

Jon-o flashed past. "Right on, little brother," he called.

The approval in his voice thrilled Wally even as he realized that the skateboard was back in the garage where he'd left it. He wasn't seeing a real ghost, just a memory tossed up from the rich store Jon-o had given him. A surge of energy filled Wally. He could do it, he thought. If he could keep his brother's spirit that vividly alive, then he was strong enough to stretch to meet the future, strong enough to be the loving man his brother would have been.

"I'm happy," Wally said in surprise. "Mom, Jon-o's dead, and I can still be happy."

His discovery made her smile. Like Jon-o, he could make her smile.